SCORCHED SKIN KILLER

A chilling crime thriller with a stunning final twist

EMMY ELLIS

DI Bethany Smith Book 4

Originally published as *How Skin Burns*

JOFFE BOOKS

Revised edition 2023
Joffe Books, London
www.joffebooks.com

First published in Great Britain in 2019
as *How Skin Burns*

This paperback edition was first published
in Great Britain in 2023

Cover art by Dee Dee Book Covers

ISBN: 978-1-83526-117-0

For the real Claire Ellis

PROLOGUE

Hell. That was life on Earth.
Secretly lethal. Evil.

Andrew held Claire's knickers up to his face, the cotton soft, red, the colour of sin. Of danger. A small green ribbon on the front matched the holly leaves all over the fabric, the hue of jealousy, envy. And he was both of those things. Jealous of the time she gave others, barely acknowledging him if she could get away with it. Envious of the clothing that got to touch her, be as close as anything could be to a person.

Someone had given her the knickers as a gift last Christmas. A joke to laugh at. He knew — he'd been listening with a glass pressed to the living room wall. She'd still put them on until recently, even though the air was full of spring with its warmer breezes and the scent of daffodils, their yellow heads bobbing in her back garden. She sat out there now, with one of her many stylish handbags on the glass-topped table, her Kindle all but pressed to her nose. Always reading, she was, distracted by fictional worlds whenever he went out to talk to her over the fence.

He'd filched the knickers off her washing line last week, same as he'd done many times before. She'd complained about it to her dad when he'd visited her once, her voice sailing through Andrew's open kitchen window from where they'd stood on her patio with its pretty flowerpots full of velvet-petaled blooms.

"I swear to God it's that weirdo from next door," she'd said.

His neck hairs had risen at that. *Weirdo.* Names burned, like skin did in the sun.

"He climbs over the fence to chat, you know, even when I don't want him near me. Even when I say no. I'm bloody sick of him. It's making me not want to go out in the garden."

"That dickhead needs talking to," her dad had said. "I'll go round there now. This has got to stop. You're a prisoner in your own home because of him."

"No," she'd said. "Leave it. He's so odd he might do something. I don't know, he could get funny."

"True. I forgot to tell you . . . Last time I came here, he was walking up and down his path in dirty underpants. Out the *front.* Who does that?" The father had clearly been grossed out.

"Don't . . ." She'd retched. That was what it had sounded like anyway. "I've seen them more often than I'd like. He's filthy."

Andrew glanced at his pants now, the only thing he had on. They weren't too bad. He didn't know what their problem was. He shrugged and placed her knickers in the drawer where he kept all the others, smoothing them out, kissing his fingertip then pressing it to the green bow. Maybe he'd steal a bra next, or that sparkly black top she liked to go out in with her friends.

Or maybe he'd steal her.

Claire Ellis. You belong to me.

CHAPTER ONE

Today it seemed winter had finally got the message to eff off. The evil chill of the wretched season had vanished, replaced by blue skies, puffy white clouds and the sense that life could finally begin again. Bethany no longer felt guilty about being alive without her husband, Vinny. She'd live how he'd want her to, as happy as she could be. That summer two years ago, his death had ripped her apart, and slowly, month by month, she'd been coping and getting better. Mike, her work partner, had moved in with her for company and to help her heal, then, a year later, had left, saying she wasn't broken anymore and didn't need him as the glue to hold her shattered pieces together.

She breathed in fresh air laced with the scent of recently cut grass, the nearby field a vast plain that stretched to the left beyond trees sprouting new leaf growth. A rambler's paradise, this, the area public woodland with tracks worn into the ground from many feet and paws that had walked through over the years. It was half a mile or so from Shadwell Hill, where her last big case had begun. She shuddered at the memory of the hole that had been dug to imprison Margaret Allthrop, then recalled the grave the woman had been placed into.

Much like this one here. Shallow, according to Isabelle, the lead SOCO.

Bethany wouldn't know. She hadn't looked at it yet, purposely averting her gaze, and she'd remained standing by the tent opening instead of going inside. When she *did* see what was in front of them, it'd take the prettiness out of the day, so she'd put it off. They stood in a clearing amongst trees, one of the main walking tracks to their right on the other side of a row of sentry-like trunks.

"What have we got?" she asked Isabelle. It was time to get on with the job and face whatever was coming their way. With them all dressed in protective clothing, there was no time like the present.

"A fresh burial," Isabelle said, kneeling beside the body. "Well, you know what I mean. She isn't rotting, put it that way. Sodding well come in, will you? She's not going to bite."

Mike cleared his throat. "Poor cow."

They entered the tent.

"Hmm." Isabelle nodded. "Not every day you find someone who's been put inside a massive plastic bag, is it."

Bethany shuddered and gave the body her attention. Yes, it certainly had been placed in transparent plastic, the victim beneath staring through it at them, unseeing, eyes a startling blue, her long blonde hair squashed against the cover in wavy swirls. A green cable tie had been used to close the bag with a plastic sprig of holly attached to it, complete with three red berries. A green bow created from once-shiny ribbon, now dulled by the filth of mud, finished off the fastening, and it was altogether too bizarre.

"Are they saying she's a Christmas present?" Bethany mused.

"Seems like it." Isabelle used a special brush to swipe away some remaining dirt. "Or they just happen to like holly. Bloody freaks, the people who do this sort of shit."

Bethany didn't disagree. "When can the bag be opened?"

"I can get that sorted now. We've been here for hours before you arrived, as you know — no point in you two coming out to stand here like lemons while we remove the mud. Everything's done that needs doing, so the next step is seeing if she's got ID on her."

"Fran's been on to missing persons. We've got thirteen possibles." Bethany turned to Mike. "If we don't know who she is, that's going to be one hell of a job for us, contacting the families of the thirteen. This might be their relation, and all prayers for one household have been ignored because this lady isn't going home safe and sound."

He sighed. "Look at it this way. That's twelve families who can still keep praying that one day their daughter, wife, or whatever, will come walking through the door."

Bethany smiled. As per usual, he found a bright side, something positive. He'd carried her through the darkest period of her life that way, always there with his shoulder to cry on and his wise words. He really was her best friend. She was bloody lucky to have him.

"Right, I'll just get the photographer back here," Isabelle said.

She called out, and the man in question ambled into the tent. They stepped back while Isabelle used a craft knife to slit the plastic down the middle, then the pictures were taken. Bethany walked out, moving to stand on the track where SOCO were getting a cast of a tyre track. Mike joined her, and they stared ahead towards the road they'd come in on.

"Reckon they brought her in this way?" he asked.

"It's closest to the main road, so probably. A quick in and out. Less chance of being spotted. If they came from the other direction, country lane, less traffic . . . Hmm, that might have worked better for them. Or they came in one side, went out the other."

"Whatever, it's going to take a lot of searching on the evidence front." He used his wrist to lower his face mask.

There were several other SOCOs already spread out, some walking slowly step by step, others on hands and knees in a line. A few uniforms helped, and about five hundred metres ahead at the beginning of the track, Tory Yates did her usual, standing guard with the scene log. Out on the verge, Glen Underby stopped traffic and asked each driver questions: *Did you see anything suspicious? Do you use this road at night or during the early hours of the morning?* Another uniform did the same on the lane out the back.

A mammoth operation, whichever way you looked at it. Loads of man hours, the budget right up the swanny. Chief Kribbs whinging about costs and whatnot: *Let's catch this person as quickly as possible, please, team.*

Sir, we'll catch them when we bloody catch them.

The sound of the camera lens whirring stopped. Bethany and Mike returned to the tent. The bag had been drawn away to rest either side of the woman. Isabelle got down on her knees and glanced over at them.

"What the chuffing hell has she got on?" Isabelle said.

Bethany studied the dress. Black, a high neck with frills on the edge, like some kind of Victorian effort. Silk, by the look of it. One of the sleeves had a long rip in it, jagged, as though it had caught on something sharp and torn, the top edge lying over the other. Had that happened when the body was being taken out of a vehicle? Numerous buttons marched up the middle of the bodice, close together. There had to be about fifty of them, fabric-covered and small. It would have taken ages to do them all up, so someone had time on their hands and hadn't been in any rush.

"Looks like something from the olden days." Bethany whipped her phone out and sent Fran a message.

Bethany: CHECK ONLINE WHERE YOU CAN BUY THIS SORT OF DRESS. IMAGE INCOMING. SORRY, BUT THERE'S A BODY WITH IT.

Fran: OKAY. IS IT BAD? THE BODY, I MEAN.

Bethany: THERE'S NO BLOOD OR BRUISING, IF THAT'S WHAT YOU'RE WORRIED ABOUT SEEING.

Fran: GOOD.

Bethany snapped a picture then sent it along. Leona was already busy with CCTV, looking for vehicles that had come close to the area. She'd deal with speaking to the owners and verifying alibis.

The victim's face was perfect — like Bethany had said to Fran, no blood, no bruising. Pale skin, no makeup, and if it wasn't for the plastic bag messing her hair up, that would have been nice, too. It appeared as if she took care of it with regular cuts and colour — no split ends or dark roots. If she'd been abducted, she hadn't been kept for long. The dress was creepy, though, giving her a governess feel, with the illusion that she was stern a falsehood, and all because of the outfit. Clothes, in this case, didn't maketh the woman.

The rumble of a vehicle broke her contemplation, and Bethany looked over her shoulder, out of the tent flap at the trees behind. Between two trunks, she made out Presley, the ME, coming towards them in his red car, his promise of being with them inside half an hour kept. While he parked down the way and suited up, Bethany continued her perusal of the corpse, taking interest in her shoes. Well, they were boots, again Victorian, with buttons down the sides and toilet pedestal heels. Black leather. Modern replicas were available in shops and on the 'net, so searching for those purchases would take time they didn't have if they wanted to solve this quickly.

Shit.

Presley came abreast of them. "Afternoon."

Hellos out of the way, Bethany said, "Is it just me, or does this make anyone else uncomfortable? The way she's dressed. It's just the weirdest thing."

"What, weirder than the clown makeup in the garden case?" Isabelle shook her head. "I don't think anything will beat that for me."

"It's still the Dyson that gives me chills," Mike said, referring to the Bishway case.

"I know what you're saying," Bethany said, "but this is unsettling, like the woman has walked out of another time and into this one. I can't explain it — it's as if she doesn't belong."

"Well, she hasn't walked out of a bloody time pocket from the past to now." Isabelle moved the skirt to check beneath the fabric. "Ah, a bag."

It was more like a pouch, black again, with a drawstring, a larger version of the velvet ones used for diamonds in all those heist films. Isabelle opened it carefully and withdrew a card.

"Driver's licence?" Bethany asked.

"Yes, but it's been butchered." Isabelle held it out so they could see.

Bethany and Mike stepped closer. The victim's information was there, but her photo had been blacked out with what Bethany guessed was a Sharpie. Written beneath was: HOW SKIN BURNS. What the hell did *that* mean? She shuddered and messaged Fran the woman's name and address — Helen Chown, thirty-seven Potter's Yard — and asked her to get on with finding the next of kin then make a start on poking into Helen's past.

"Anything else in that bag?" Bethany lowered her mask.

"Nothing." Isabelle stood and placed the licence and pouch in separate evidence bags, handing them off to a colleague. "She's yours for the perusing," she said to Presley.

He'd been sketching the body's position on his scene form. With a scribble of words at the bottom, he popped it in his bag, taking it with him to kneel beside the body. "I'm going to do an ear temp — at least she's got some dignity with that."

Taking the rectal temp wasn't something Bethany was comfortable with watching, so she was relieved about Presley's decision. While no one here would take any notice of Presley working, there were so many officers around, she understood his reasoning. Just because Helen was dead, didn't mean they should treat her without respect. To be fair, Bethany wasn't happy with *any* of this — the location, the clothing, the face being blacked out on the licence. Those words.

"Um, you might want to come round here and look at this," Presley said.

"What . . ." Cautious, Bethany remained where she was.

"I've just brushed against her sleeve," he said. "Come and see."

Bethany and Mike moved to stand behind him. The rip in the material gaped open, revealing scorched skin on the upper arm, scabs where it had begun the healing process, and several areas where it peeled like sunburn, although the latter appeared to have been pulled off, leaving a faint wiggly edge, like a coastline or a saltwater mark on suede shoes.

"So she was near fire?" Bethany said.

"Or concentrated heat." Presley took his eyeglass out and peered through it. "There's been significant warmth, at a high degree, in patches. If you look at the scabs, they're circular, thicker in the centre and raised, so I'd say a tool that produces heat. A blowtorch, maybe a branding iron."

"Christ," Mike said. "And if there's scabs, that was inflicted on her when she was alive. What the hell?"

"Correct." Presley nodded. "Incredibly painful. There are four scabs, and the surrounding skin has been burnt, but less, and more in keeping with how you'd burn in the sun. Now, I'm going to put it out there that the scabs were originally blisters. They would have been large, think tennis balls, the skin stretched and yellow, filled with pus, and the blisters would have popped and—"

"Nope, no more." Bethany held up her hand to stop him; she couldn't listen to it any longer. She imagined the rest of the body like this, the evidence of torture hidden by a sinister dress.

"The skin, the paper-thin bits that would naturally peel with sunburn, have been pulled off," Presley went on. "Otherwise, there'd be large flakes ready for picking."

"God." Mike shook his head. "She'd been kept somewhere, no question about that. This would take time — the burning of the skin, the wait for the scabs to form."

"That narrows down our thirteen AWOL women. Some of them might not have been missing for long enough." Bethany sighed. "We'd be looking at how far back, Pres?"

"Those scabs are about a week old." He got a little metal tool out and tapped it on a scab. "Hear that? Rock-hard."

Bethany shivered at the noise it had made. "Did you have to do that?"

"No, but I did." He smiled. "It's my little way of working out the depth of a scab. The centres are about five to ten millimetres, I'd say. Savage wounds to have crusts like these."

"Her temperature?" Bethany asked to change the subject.

"She's been dead only a couple of days, so burial was recent," Presley said.

"So she could even have been buried last night?"

Isabelle nodded. "I'd agree with that. The earth covering her wasn't compact enough. They'd only lightly patted the top down and covered it with grass clippings from the adjacent field."

"Any handprints regarding the patting?" Bethany could only hope.

"No. V-shaped lines were present, probably from the end of a pointed shovel."

"Right, so they dug the grave themselves, not with machinery," Bethany said. "I see a cast is being taken, looked like a tyre mark to me, so a vehicle parked on the track. Bit stupid, don't you reckon? Okay, they'd have undoubtedly been here during the night, so other people wouldn't have been around, but you'd think they'd have driven closer — you could easily fit a van through those two trees there." She pointed at them. "People camp out here. Whoever it was risked being spotted."

"Maybe they did a recon beforehand," Mike said. "I would, if it were me."

"It takes time to dig a grave," Bethany said. "With the earth hard from winter . . ."

"We had a shedload of rain the past two days, don't forget." Presley used his tool to poke it into the ground an arm's length away from the body. It went in easily. "It wouldn't have taken as long as you think. An hour or so, perhaps two if the mud was harder farther down. If you've got a sharp shovel . . ."

"Hmm." Bethany imagined the scene: Park up. Leave the body in the vehicle. Come across into the trees to dig. It brought something to mind. "Any footprints in the surrounding area?"

Isabelle shook her head. "Seemed they used a rake, can you believe, to smooth it over. They knew what they were doing. To have brought such a thing with them, they've clearly thought about it for a while. You can see them sitting there planning it, can't you, writing down what they need to do to remove evidence."

"There'll be something on her," Presley said. "Fibres, whatever. The body talks after death."

That sounded eerie, and again, Bethany shivered. This whole scenario creeped her out. What was the Victorian angle all about? And why had Helen been burnt?

"She's got a contusion on the back of her head," Presley informed them.

Bethany's phone went off — Fran with the next of kin details.

"We have to go."

Bethany said goodbye and went with Mike out onto the track. They walked towards Presley's car which he'd parked a fair way down so as not to contaminate the scene, behind crime tape strung up from trees on either side. She ducked under it and continued to the road, her head bent, scouring the ground, even though it had already been done, hoping to find something for them to go on.

Standing beside Tory, Bethany said, "Anything here?"

Tory shook her head. "Glen's had nothing from drivers. I've been sending all the licence plates to Leona."

"Thanks. Well, we'd better be off. How long have you been here?"

"My shift ends in three hours. I'll stay until then, if you like."

"Please. It'll be around then that the body can be moved."

"God, this part of the job . . ." Tory's lip wobbled.

Bethany patted Tory's shoulder. "I know, love. I know."

CHAPTER TWO

Claire looked through her kitchen window and out into the back garden. Andrew was in his, prancing about with his arms spread, fingers splayed, again in just his dirty underpants. They must have been white once. Now a sickly grey, they sported the usual brown blemishes. He sickened her — frightened her at times, if she were honest — but when she'd complained to the police about him, they'd told her that unless he threatened or harmed her, there was nothing they could do except ask him not to come into her garden.

He'd ignored their request to respect her privacy, nipping over her fence to steal her knickers again. She'd taken to hanging them indoors on the clothes airer instead. The thought of him having her underwear sent her cold.

She'd contemplated a restraining order, but how could that work when they lived next door to each other? Not coming within a certain distance of her wasn't feasible. She'd have to give in and put up a higher fence. Dad had already said he'd do it for her in the summer when he had some time off work. Until then, she'd just have to put up with that creepy twat invading her space.

It was a lovely day, so warm for the beginning of spring, as though a switch had been flicked and they'd gone from cold to cheery in an instant. She was dying to sit outside and read. It didn't look like Andrew was going in any time soon, though, but why should she stand here waiting for him to leave? Why did she even have to contemplate what she did? It was *her* garden, and she should be able to sit in it without interruptions.

Sod it. She was going out there.

She grabbed her latest new handbag, a nice purple one from eBay. It contained her drink bottle, Kindle, a couple of snacks, and her phone — it saved her having to get up and down going in and out of the house when she needed something. She opened the door, holding her breath, waiting for him to start his incessant jabbering. Just anticipating his voice set her nerves on edge.

Andrew stopped weaving around and immediately came over to the dividing fence, staying on his side. Claire clenched her teeth until it hurt — God, she bloody *hated* him. He unsettled her, invaded her life and mind far too often, infecting her sense of well-being. How do you tell someone to fuck off without actually saying it? She hated to be rude, it wasn't in her nature, but she might have to be to get through to him.

Right. She could do this. She'd pretend he wasn't even there, act as though she couldn't see or hear him. He had to learn that this was *her* space, her time to relax, and that he wasn't welcome to encroach on it by hanging over the fucking fence and trying to engage her in his banal style of conversation. If she was lucky, she'd get right into the current book she had on the go and not hear him. It was a tongue-in-cheek guide: *One Hundred Ways to Kill Thy Neighbour.*

If only she could get away with that.

She got herself settled in her chair and popped her bag on the table. The afternoon sun beamed down, warming her little garden. Kindle out, she opened the book and scrolled to the cover. Then she propped the Kindle against her bag and took a picture for her Facebook group, Books & Bags. It was a friendly community of women who loved reading and also had a passion for handbags. She ran quarterly book exchanges, where each member sent another a book, plus some goodies to brighten their days — bookmarks, chocolates, nice little postcards. It was a haven, somewhere to go online and be free of that prat who now drummed his fingertips on the top of the fence.

"Why do you always take pictures of what you're reading?" he asked, his voice nasal and whiny.

Claire ignored him and got comfy, then held her Kindle up so he couldn't see her face and, hopefully, would get the message that she was blocking him from sight. She tuned out his heavy breathing and concentrated on reading from where she'd left off this morning.

SCENARIO ONE

Necessity: Single occupant, because subduing innocent parties prior to the main event takes up too much time and increases your risk of being caught.

Let's begin!

So you've had enough, right? Your neighbour is an absolute nightmare. No matter how you've tried to resolve things in the past, they continue to annoy you. They may know your feelings regarding them, or you may have kept them simmering inside and smiled each time you approached them to get disputes sorted. Either way, they have to be stopped.

With all other avenues exhausted, there's nothing left but murder.

Imagine this . . .

Creep into your neighbour's house at night, using their key — after all, you know where they keep the spare, don't you? Beneath the gnome or in the fake rock from Home Bargains, or on the back door lintel, even amidst the shingled flowerbeds or under the recycle bin. If you're still acting super-friendly with them — a good ruse as it takes suspicion off you (see the 'highly recommended' tips at the end of the book) — you can even take a key off their hallway table when you nip to the loo between drinking cuppas and eating their chocolate Hobnobs — they owe you those Hobnobs for putting you through shit, damn it!

By whatever means — GET THAT KEY.

You've lived there long enough to know their movements, their habits, and what time they go to bed. Let's say it's ten o'clock. Wait until eleven or, preferably, much later, giving them plenty of time to nod off, and for the love of God, make sure their light is off and there's no blue glow from a television. No rookie mistakes allowed here! Of course, if they have an alarm system, that makes things more difficult, but we'll cover that later.

For now, we'll assume they haven't got one.

For now, we're just dreaming of being able to do this.

Anything to get you through the day.

Once you're inside, remember the rules from earlier:

GLOVES.

SHOWER CAPS OVER YOUR SHOES.

HAIRNET.

PAPER BOILER SUIT.

FACE MASK. *(A full one that goes over your head. Why not buy a creepy sort for the fun of it? Perhaps a pig or a ghost. There's nothing like scaring the crap out of your neighbour just before you bump them off. The memories of their reaction will give you hours of entertainment in the years to come while you eat those Hobnobs that will forever remind you of this momentous time in your life.)*

PURCHASE THE ABOVE GOODS WITH CASH, MONTHS BEFORE THE EVENT, AND NOT IN YOUR HOMETOWN. DO NOT USE THE INTERNET.

Your body must be covered as much as possible — we don't want any slipups in the evidence department, do we? Have you got the large metal bucket or other non-melting receptacle ready in your back garden? You'll need to put all those items in it and burn them. After that, you'll have to dispose of the ashes, but again, that's a topic to be discussed later. We just want to get straight to the meat of it — the murder!

Now, ensure you are not seen by other neighbours when you enter the house. This is a given, but it bears saying anyway. You wouldn't believe the amount of people who don't do this crucial step. Nosy Nelly could be closing her curtains and spot you. Complaining Carol could be getting home late from using the only payphone left in town to leave an anonymous message on the council's answering machine. She called them about Vicious Vera's irritating habit of filling everyone else's wheelie bins with her rubbish, which contains glass, for God's sake — she's too lazy to take it to the bottle bank; the nerve of the woman. My point: You could be seen.

Enter the house — quietly, none of that bumbling around and knocking into things. This folly could wake your quarry, and really, that's the last thing you need. Stand in their hallway and listen to the sounds of a house settling for the night — the whir of the fridge, the clank of the central heating pipe, the excited breathing coming in and out of you. Feel the buzz of anticipation in the air. Gather your mettle. Ensure your weapon of choice is close to hand. Let's choose a meat cleaver in this instance. One jolly good chop to the neck should sort any worries about your neighbour making a racket. They'll be startled awake and stare at you, gurgling, frightened quicker into death by the mask. What a hoot!

"Did you hear what I just said?" Andrew shouted.

Claire had been deep into the scenario, seeing herself in those clothes, standing at the bottom of Andrew's stairs, the cleaver clutched in her fist. A thrill had gone through her at the thought of bringing it down on his neck, blood spurting, his weird, raspy voice cut off forever, body writhing then twitching as his life seeped away, so much redness staining the sheets.

She didn't have the inclination to respond to him so stared at the words on her screen.

Climb the stairs. Make sure you do this carefully — we don't want any creaks to alert your neighbour that someone is in the house. They could be one of those inconvenient light sleepers — bloody cheek!

"I was in a play by George Bernard Shaw," Andrew called out. "I miss those days."

Claire couldn't imagine him acting, but the dancing, yes. That must be why he floated around in his garden — he was reliving his stage days. She had no idea when he'd been in that play. He'd probably told her when she'd been engrossed in her book.

"Do you like plays, Claire?" he asked.

She kept the Kindle up at her face.

You're at the bedroom door. It's closed, but that's okay. You open it, push it wide, and stand inside the frame, a person intent on ridding yourself of the scum you've had to live near for too long. They're on their back, in the perfect position for you to arc that cleaver through the air and back into their throat.

"Claire, I *said*, do you like plays? Why won't you answer me?"

You move to the side of the bed and stare down at the person who's annoyed you, hurt you, had you going out of your mind with irritation. Everything bubbles up, a cauldron of boiling spite, and you lift that cleaver. It glints from the shaft of moonlight coming in through the gap in the curtains, and it's so clean, but soon . . . soon it'll be covered in claret.

"Claire!" he whispered.

Hot air fanned her cheek.

He was beside her, his filthy pants level with her face. She squealed and jumped up, backing away, her heart beating too fast. He'd climbed the fence again, and God, she was just about ready to dive inside and pick up her own cleaver to embed it in his skull.

"Get out," she said, staring at him. "Get out of my fucking garden or I'm going to call the police."

He stepped towards her. "Why are you mean to me, Claire? What have I ever done to you?" He raised a hand, dramatic, his face contorted by confusion.

He wasn't right in the head, and she saw that now. She'd suspected that in the past, but here, this minute, it was plain he had a screw loose. He needed help, but so did she — help in getting him to understand he shouldn't be in her garden.

"I'm warning you," she said, "if you don't get out now . . ."

"Holly loves the drawer," he said, walking backwards.

What is he on about?

She shivered. Waited for him to climb back over. Then she sat, refusing to be forced inside like so many times before. She'd read with her Kindle resting on her lap so she could detect any movement from him. The second he went to vault the fence again, she was calling nine-nine-nine. She'd put up with him no more. Her limit had been reached.

"I'll put on a play for you, Claire," he said. "You'll have a part in it. I'll find you a pretty dress."

"I don't want to be in a bloody play," she said, the words spilling before she could stop herself. Engaging with him was encouragement for him to keep pestering her. *Shit.*

"You won't have a choice," he whispered.

"Excuse me?" That was a threat. Her insides seemed to hollow, leaving her weak and shaking. "*What* did you just say to me?" She'd sounded stronger than she felt, thank goodness. She didn't want him knowing he scared her sometimes.

"I said: I'm sure you have a lovely singing voice."

He hadn't said that, not at all, but she wouldn't argue with him about it. That would mean he had her attention, something he didn't deserve. She lowered her head to stare at the words on her screen. He was in her periphery, so that was okay. She had time to bolt into the house if he decided to come onto her property for a second time today.

And you swing that blade down, chopping so far in you almost reach the other side. A reflexive eye-opening from your victim has you thinking they know it's you behind the mask, and it gives you satisfaction that finally, you have the upper hand, the last laugh. You would laugh, too, but the neighbours on the other side might hear you through the wall, so you keep it all inside. Your skin, it's so hot behind the rubber — watch the sweat, you don't want to leave a single part of you behind.

You back out, onto the landing, and watch the spreading bloodstain for a moment. Then look down at yourself to check the state of the boiler suit. Splashes of black that in light would be crimson. Careful, careful now, you don't want to touch the banister rail or the walls on your way downstairs. Out of the house you go, back to yours, and you'd better hope Nelly, Carol, or Vera aren't keeping tabs. Quickly, into your garden. Remove the boiler suit, mindful you don't get blood on your clothes. Set fire to the petrol-soaked rags in the bucket. Add your items one by one.

Tomorrow, the ashes can be put inside a paper bag. You'll take them to a remote place and scatter them, then burn the bag. In the woods, by a river, somewhere no one goes. Then, once the police come round — and they will — you must act shocked, perhaps cry for good measure. "Oh, my poor neighbour! Who would do such a thing?"

Who indeed . . .

"And I think it would be best if we rehearse three nights a week," Andrew said.

She raised her eyes a bit so it looked like she was still reading, but she was watching him instead. He had his eyes closed and . . . was he rubbing himself against the fence? He gripped the top, knuckles prominent, the skin stretched, and her stomach churned at the sight of him getting off — there was nothing else to call it. She grabbed her phone and videoed him. If the police didn't think this was something to worry about, she didn't know what else to do.

Andrew grunted and moved from side to side, the fence juddering.

"I'll take you *there*," he said. "Oh, how skin burns."

He was talking in riddles. Where did he want to take her? And what did burning skin have to do with anything? He was a fucking psycho. No longer able to sit outside — fear had got its teeth right into her after all — she continued filming and, in reverse, went into her house, locking the door.

Andrew gyrated for a few more seconds, shuddered, then snapped his eyes open, a puzzled expression forming at the sight of her empty chair. She quickly stepped into the shadows of the room — he wouldn't see her there. She'd checked before how much of her kitchen was visible from the fence.

"The black one," he shouted. "I want the black one next."

She shivered. What was he talking about? He didn't make any sense half the time, yet others, he was lucid and could hold a normal conversation.

Claire made a decision then. As well as a taller fence, she'd get a camera fitted to record the garden at all times. One with sound so it picked up his weird ramblings. Him saying she didn't have a choice about doing a play frightened her. She couldn't sit by and allow him to intimidate her anymore. If the police weren't going to do anything about him, she'd just have to do it her bloody self.

CHAPTER THREE

The drama society gave Andrew something to look forward to. He was a loner out there in the world, but in the community centre where they practised, and on the stage, he was someone else entirely. Gone was the past, the unsettling memories, and in their place came contentment and happiness. Stacey Maxey, their director, was like that woman, a reminder of the past. Same as his neighbour, Claire. It was the blonde hair and blue eyes, he reckoned.

All the others had gone home after they'd done a dress rehearsal for the George Bernard Shaw play. Stacey's black Victorian dress fitted her perfectly, its high neck obscuring her slender throat, the ruffles at the top of it level with her jaw.

It was just like that other dress . . .

He'd imagined wrapping his hands around Stacey's neck once, squeezing until all the breath left her lungs, until her lips turned blue and her eyes bulged. It had only been a fleeting visual, but it had revved him up all the same. Got him going good and proper. He'd had to hide the tent in his trousers.

"I'm just going to get out of this thing," Stacey said. "It itches like mad."

Off she went, through a doorway, and he entertained thoughts of her in a toilet cubicle, lifting that black silk above her head, exposing her breasts encased in a lacy bra.

He stripped where he was, quickly, in case the caretaker came in, then put his usual clothes on, covering up the pants he yet again hadn't changed. He folded the costume neatly, placing it in the box of outfits, a thrill going through him that Stacey's dress would be next in the pile — her on top of him, so to speak.

His dick played up at that.

Stacey came back in, and he stared while she popped the dress in the box. He'd bet the material whiffed of her perfume. She came over, her vest top showing her sunburnt arms, the skin peeling in places. On her shoulders, too. It had been a pretty warm summer.

She caught him looking and blushed.

"I forgot sun cream while I was on holiday," she said by way of explanation and plopped herself down on the edge of the stage. Then she picked the flakes of skin. A lot of it came off in sheets, sailing to the floor, tissue paper in the wind.

Mesmerised, he watched, rapt, wishing he was that skin, touched by her but not discarded. She talked about her work, how so-and-so had broken the kettle so they'd been gasping for a cuppa until the boss had gone to Argos and bought a new one. What a mad day!

Andrew responded with appropriate noises and a few "Oh dear!", and she seemed content to waffle on without much input from him.

She'd pulled a fair lot of skin off one arm and shoulder then started on the next, all the while nattering about her dog, Miss Aphrodite, a Great Dane that slobbered everywhere but was so good on the lead when out walking.

Andrew could listen to Stacey all day.

A good half hour must have passed and, once she'd finished shedding, she got up and thanked him for the chat, then left, without so much as an offer to give him a lift home. He was a bit put out by that — she always *gave him a lift. It was what he looked forward to most throughout the week.*

The breeze from the door closing shifted all her skin, sending it towards the base of the stage, where it gathered in a cream line. He took one of the notices off the corkboard — COME TO KARATE AND LEARN TO DEFEND YOURSELF! *— and scooped up the parts of Stacey. Sniffed them.*

Paper folded so the skin couldn't escape, he popped it in his pocket and walked out, saying goodbye to the caretaker along the way. The journey home was all right, and he thought about his wall and how pretty it would look once his project was complete. Eager to continue with it, he slid the key in his front door and turned it. Claire from next door appeared on her step, her sparkly black top suggesting that she was going out for a drink. It was quiz night after all, and he almost asked her if he could go with her, but he had an idea she knew he'd stolen her knickers again last week.

She gave him a filthy look as she closed her door, so yes, she knew what he'd done.

Claire tottered up the street, her high heels clacking, and he squashed the urge to follow her. He couldn't, not when he had Stacey's skin. He sighed and went inside, going straight to the spare room. The black paper silhouette of a woman greeted him, stuck to the wall, waiting for him to decorate it some more. He moved forward and studied the maps he'd drawn on it with silver pen. One was of the community centre on the left breast. The belly had a floorplan, the home of Miss Estera Zabek, and each room was filled with skin — her skin, the one who'd started his obsession with it. He'd carefully pasted on the super-fine flakes, and they'd dried against the black, the diamond-like pattern showing up as grey.

Silver pen in hand, he drew Claire's house on the right breast. Whether he filled it in with skin was up to her. If she welcomed him with open arms, did what he wanted, everything would be fine.

It was time to fill the community centre, and he hadn't even needed to burn Stacey himself to get the goods. The sun had been on his side, doing it for him.

Using tweezers to unroll some of Stacey, he placed each piece between sheets of paper then put weights on top of them. They'd be nice and flat tomorrow, dried out, too, and ready to be added to the map. Eventually, the whole of the silhouette would be covered.

He was excited about that.

CHAPTER FOUR

Fay Chown, Helen's mother, stood at her front door and smiled. That smile quickly faded once Bethany produced her ID and introduced them, saying their visit was regarding her daughter.

"Oh . . . Oh . . ." Fay stepped back then wandered off down the hallway, her short black hair skewed in all directions, and not from styling, more from fingers running through it.

Bethany glanced at Mike and they walked inside, closing the door behind them and entering the room at the end. A lounge. Fay stood at the window of the fifth-floor high-rise, staring out at a city that, at the moment, kept the secret of where Helen had been during the days since she'd gone missing. Bethany gestured at Mike for him to take a perch, and she did the same in the hope it would encourage the woman to follow their lead.

"Mrs Chown, we're here to get some information on the days prior to Helen's disappearance," Bethany said.

"I told the police this already on the phone." Fay rubbed her arms, keeping her back to them.

That was a pest. Bethany couldn't see her facial reactions to any questions.

"Please could you sit, Mrs Chown."

She did, balancing on the arm of a chair beside the fireplace.

"When did you notice Helen had gone missing?" Bethany smiled in sympathy.

"Monday last week. She was meant to have come here. She's a nail technician and had the day off. My acrylics needed doing, so she was going to sort them."

"I see. What time was she supposed to arrive?"

"About nine. She had some private clients to visit after me. One of them — a family friend — rang me to see where Helen was. She hadn't honoured the appointment. Helen wasn't answering her phone, and that's unheard of unless she's at work, and even then, she manages to sneak in a quick call or respond to messages every so often. She didn't answer on the Tuesday either."

"What did you do then?"

"I drove round to her flat. She didn't open the door, so I went in — I've got an emergency key, and sometimes I pop in there to give the place a bit of a clean if she's done overtime or whatever. She works so hard, and we all know housework is the last thing on our minds after a long week. I only do half days, see, so I've got the time and energy to help her out."

"What was her flat like when you went in?" Bethany was after signs of a struggle, an abduction.

"The usual. A few dishes in the sink, an overflowing laundry bin, so I took it all and brought it home."

"You did her washing . . . ?"

"I did. Still got it here."

Bethany could scream. Those clothes might have held vital evidence before they'd been through the bloody machine, doused in Persil or whatever. She held in a sigh. "Okay, so nothing seemed untoward there?"

"No. I was bored so cleaned up."

Oh, give me strength . . . Okay, this woman was just being a good mother and had no idea the flat could be a crime scene, but this had buggered it up for forensics. "What level of cleaning did you do?"

"Oh, I went to town. Bleached, polished, the lot. She hadn't made her bed, so I changed the sheets and whatnot."

Fuck it.

"It took my mind off . . . well, Helen not answering my calls." Fay shrugged. "I'd phoned her work on the Tuesday as well, and Helen hadn't gone in. That was when I rang the police, and I have to say, no disrespect to you, but they didn't seem bothered in the slightest. Waffled on about forty-eight hours, and then when that had passed and I rang again, I was sent to missing persons. In all fairness, the lady who came out to me was lovely, and she said to give it another week, then if Helen wasn't back, she'd arrange for the police to go to her flat and have a look round, just in case, you know, something happened there." She winced. "Is that why you're here? Do you need the keys?"

"That would be helpful, yes," Bethany said.

Fay went to a sideboard and took a bunch out, handing them over on her way back to her seat.

"Has Helen ever gone missing before?"

"God, no. She rings me twice a week and messages every day, at least once, and she's on that Facebook, so I can see what she's up to on there. Nothing since last Sunday night. She put up one of them memes. It's been . . . so weird without hearing from her. I'm frightened."

Bethany's heart went out to her. It must be a mother's worst nightmare, this.

"Was Helen seeing anyone?" Mike asked, pen poised over his notebook.

Fay shook her head. "No — well, not that I know of. She usually tells me when she has a fella. Sends pictures to see if I think they have dodgy eyes. She's got a thing about that."

"What about friends? Would she have gone to stay with them?" Mike jotted a few words down.

"I doubt it. They all live in Shadwell. Why stay at theirs when you have a flat here yourself? Doesn't make sense. She's got one best friend, Rose Harding, and she's away in Africa.

Has been for a month so far. Off on one of them safaris. I don't think she comes back until next week."

"What about other friends?" Bethany asked.

"Just the girls at work. Helen's at Tips and Talons on the Ring Road estate."

"Thank you." Bethany pushed herself to ask the next question. "Do you know of anyone who would want to harm Helen?"

Fay stared, her mouth hanging open. "My Helen? No! She's the kindest thing ever. Why would anyone want to hurt her?"

"I'm afraid a body was found this morning, and Helen's driving licence was in a bag with her."

"A body? What do you mean? Is she okay? Has she been injured? Is that why you asked if anyone would want to hurt her? They have, haven't they." She jumped up. "Which hospital is she in? She'll need me there. Let me just get my bag, and we can be off."

Bethany rose and walked over to her, placing a hand on her arm. "Please sit down, Fay." She pressed her into the chair then crouched beside it, holding the woman's hand. "It was a *body* — I'm so sorry, but Helen is dead."

Fay paled, and her eyes filled. "Wh . . . ?"

The tears came then, and her face crumpled. She covered her skewed, gaping mouth with a shaking hand, and her eyes squeezed shut, her shoulders shuddering. She gripped Bethany's hand tight to the point of pain, and Mike bowed his head, staring at the carpet, arms dangling between his legs. Bethany swallowed the lump in her throat. She remembered this moment with Vinny, when the first lightning strike of grief had hit, and she'd screamed, a great whoosh of panic engulfing her. Images of him had gone through her head, showing her how he was no longer in her life, and she'd wished time could go backwards so he could decide to have the night off instead of go to work and try to save a baby in a burning house.

Fay might be seeing the same now, her beautiful daughter smiling, her blonde hair a cloud around her face, skin perfect, not scabbed and burnt as it was on her arm. In this woman's head, her child was alive, full of vitality instead of resting in a shallow grave in a dress that was so out of place it was creepy.

Mike got up and mimed drinking. She nodded, and he walked out to make Fay some tea. She cried right up until Mike came back, then composed herself somewhat, her chest hitching with the aftereffects of sobs. Mike also handed her some kitchen roll, which Fay used to wipe her cheeks and nose before scrunching the tissue into a fist.

"Do you have anyone you'd like us to call?" Bethany asked.

"My mum. She lives four doors down at number ten."

Mike left the room again, and while he was gone, Fay sipped her tea, still clutching Bethany's hand.

"What happened to her?" she asked, gazing into space.

"We're not sure yet." And apart from the burns, that was true. "We'll know more after the post-mortem." She thought about how they hadn't checked beneath the high neck of the dress. Strangulation bruising could be lurking beneath it.

"When can I see her?"

"You can give the morgue a call and ask." She took out her business card and used a pen on the coffee table to write down Presley's name and number. "Give him until tomorrow, okay? She's still . . . still in situ."

"Where?"

"In the woods. She was buried."

Wince. "Who found her?"

"A lady called it in. She'd been walking her dog. The dog kept barking, and she noticed the mound — I'm so terribly sorry to be telling you this. I wish I could make it all go away."

Fay nodded. "I knew, you know. Knew she was gone."

"How?"

Fay pressed a hand to her chest. "In here. Sunday night, it was. I had a dreadful feeling but brushed it off. Told myself not to be so silly. I was going to message her . . . but decided not to. She'd only have said I was daft."

Bethany had heard many a mother say they knew. The bond was somehow spiritual, she reckoned, like some kind of connective energy alerting a mum that something was wrong. A feeling brought on by the child being in danger or imminent death looming on the horizon.

Mike came back then, an elderly woman in tow, and after making sure Fay would be okay — she didn't want Alice Jacobs, the FLO — and taking Fay's phone number, they left, Helen's keys firmly in Bethany's pocket. In the car, she rang Isabelle and arranged for some of her team to meet them at the flat.

"I forgot to ask Presley to look at Helen's neck while we were there," Bethany said to her.

"Ah, yes, we did that after you'd gone. No sign of strangulation. We undid the dress buttons — single stab wound to the torso, which was a mass of blisters, scabs, and burns." Isabelle sighed.

"Oh, fucking hell . . ."

"I know. She went through it before death, and I imagine dying was a blessing come the end. She had to have been in terrible pain."

"Just awful. We've been to see the mother. She had a sixth sense, knew something was wrong."

"Poor thing. Okay, I'm basically done here so I'll draft in a couple of others who haven't been on shift today. This lot are knackered but are staying on to check if there are older graves — you just never know. See you at the flat."

Bethany tucked her phone away and drove to Potter's Yard, which had literally been such a thing many years ago. A pottery barn had created beautiful tableware from the twenties to the eighties, but once the cheaper items became available elsewhere, the place had gone out of business. Now, it was a courtyard with flats on three sides, a horseshoe, two-storey housing that mimicked an older style but were actually new builds. She imagined they'd be expensive to buy. How had Helen afforded it? Or had she rented?

They parked closest to thirty-seven and suited up while they waited for Isabelle. She turned up with her team twenty minutes later, Isabelle looking drained, her colleagues fresh and rested. Helen's flat was on the ground floor, so Bethany opened the door and let the team in. Isabelle went next, and while she did the first inspection, Bethany and Mike stood outside.

Isabelle returned, standing on the doorstep. "It's clean as a whistle — and I'm talking obsessively clean. That's dodgy. Someone's—"

"Her mother did it last Tuesday," Bethany said. "She popped round here to see if Helen was home, saw it was a bit messy, and did her usual cleaning stint. She helped her daughter out from time to time. It's a ball-ache, but there's nothing we can do about it now."

"Let's just hope her mother missed some nooks and crannies then. We might find something. Come and see for yourself. If it wasn't such a crass thing to do, I'd ask her mother to be my cleaner. That woman has a gift."

Bethany and Mike chuckled, following Isabelle inside. And yes, Fay definitely had a gift. Spotless. No sneaky cobwebs lurking in corners, not a speck of anything on the floors. The kitchen gleamed, and all the curtains had been opened, the pleats exact. The fact that Helen would never come in here and see how much care her mum had put into scrubbing the place saddened Bethany. There was nothing for it but to look in drawers and whatnot to establish what kind of person Helen was and if they could find something that indicated she was having trouble with someone.

Oddly, there was no computer, laptop, or tablet in the bedroom or living room.

"That's weird," Mike said.

"I know." Bethany had a bad feeling in her gut.

"Everyone her age has some kind of computer, don't they?" he said. "So did they take it away? Were they here — as in, did they know Helen and abduct her from her flat, as well as any devices?"

"My mind is going along the same lines. We'll have to speak to the neighbours." She glanced at the clock on the wall. "That's handy. Home time for most people. Hopefully everyone will be in."

"Um, you might want to come in here," Isabelle called.

They followed her voice to the kitchen.

"Broken champagne flute in the cupboard." Isabelle pointed. "Can you ring the mother and check whether she did it?"

Mike nodded and went off to do that.

"Are there any visible fingerprints on it?" Bethany stepped closer and peered at the glass. The stem and base of the triangular bit for wine was intact, but the top had a jagged edge, as though the rim had been tapped on something and smashed. "What the fuck is that inside it?"

Isabelle smiled. "Wondered when you'd notice. Someone's cut out little flames from paper and put them in it."

"I doubt very much that was Fay Chown — her mother, by the way. Unless it's some kind of in-joke."

Mike appeared and leant on the doorframe. "She said it wasn't her, and she didn't notice it broken either."

"Okay, so we could take this as something to look into," Isabelle said. "Helen could have kept it, but that's just plain odd if she did."

"I agree." Bethany studied the flames. "Someone's taken the bloody time to draw them and colour them in with felt tips. And they've got a film on them. Something hard."

Isabelle dipped her head forward to inspect them. "Hmm, some kind of coating. We'll get them down the lab, see what comes up after testing. Can't see any fingerprints, though."

"I'd say if you're in the business of murder, gloves are at the top of your shopping list before you embark on that particular career." Bethany stretched her hands over her head, relieving some tension in her shoulders. "We've got neighbours to speak to, so we'll leave you to it. Can you get hold of me right away when you have news on those flames?"

"Will do. Probably won't be until the end of play tomorrow, the day after, even."

"Thanks."

They walked out of the flat and took off their gear, storing it in a paper bag in the boot. Splitting up, they took half the flats each, and Bethany was losing hope by the time she got to her last one. The door was opened by a young man, about twenty-three, in a grey suit, blue shirt, his stripy tie loosened at the knot.

"Yeah, there was something weird," he said. "Last Sunday night."

Bethany's stomach cramped. *Fay said Sunday* . . . "What was weird about it?"

"Must have been around one in the morning. An engine was idling for ages, so I got out of bed to look. A car was parked by number thirty-seven, backed up to the front door, the boot open. The front door was, too, but no lights were on in the flat."

"Do you remember the colour?"

"It was dark out — we've only got those two lamps by the courtyard entrance, and they're not bright. The headlights weren't on, so I couldn't even see by that."

"What happened then?"

He shrugged. "I went back to bed. I fell asleep still hearing the engine."

No one else had said anything about this to her — they'd all been asleep. Mike might have picked something up, and she'd check in with him in a minute.

"Anything else?" she asked.

"No. I don't know the woman at that address. Don't actually know anyone yet. I only came here a month ago."

"Have you seen her, though? I mean, you set up in a new place and check out other people's movements, who lives where . . ."

"Not me. I mind my own business and avoid any of that 'hello, lovely day' rubbish."

"Okay." She handed him her card. "If you remember more, give me a ring."

"Yep."

She said thank you and met Mike at the car. "Strike lucky?"

"Nope." He shook his head.

"Good job I got something then, isn't it."

While they drove back to the station to catch up with Fran and Leona, Bethany told him what the neighbour had said.

"I bet someone put her in the back of that bloody car," he said.

"Yep. And I want to know who the fuck it is, the sick bastard."

CHAPTER FIVE

Claire was livid. Earlier, Andrew had put up a tripod at the bottom of his garden with a camcorder on top — pointing directly at her bedroom window. What the hell was she supposed to do about that? Go round there and tell him to take it down? What, was he hoping to catch a glimpse of her getting undressed at night? Good job she always closed her curtains. She'd thought about it all day and planned to ring the police in the morning. Something had to be done about him. This couldn't go on.

Determined to shove it to the back of her mind for now, she put on her 'going out' top, the sparkly black one. She'd be meeting her mates later at The Lamb Shank. It was quiz night, and she'd brushed up on her Tudor studies lately — last month they'd been stumped on the name of Henry the Eighth's third wife. Bugger being caught out like that again.

She had an hour or so before she had to meet Katy and Viv, and rather than bumble around the house waiting for the clock to tick along, she decided to go to the local café and have some dinner. They did a lovely lasagne and chips, a bit of tomato, cucumber, and frilly purple lettuce on the side, which bugged her. She preferred iceberg, but you couldn't have everything, could you.

She walked out, conscious that Andrew might be lurking by his living room window, the freak. Claire purposely didn't look that way as she passed his house, head bent so he couldn't catch her eye and come racing down his path, underwear on show, to engage her in shitty conversation along with his equally shitty Y-fronts. She breathed a sigh of relief at the end of the street, turning left and heading two roads along to Bottoms Up Bistro. Inside, she ordered then got her Kindle out while she waited for her food to arrive.

SCENARIO FIFTEEN

Necessity: You must be on fake-friendly terms for this one.

Offer to take your neighbour out on a drive. At night. In the countryside.

You must research your area carefully.

This trip should be off the cuff, no chance for them to tell anyone. Spontaneity is the spice of life.

Rules:

CHECK OUT CCTV

CHOOSE COUNTRY LANES WITH MINIMAL TRAFFIC

SELECT A LOCATION OUT IN THE STICKS

CREATE AN ALIBI BEFOREHAND (Tell a friend you're ill, which means an early night — you'll be using your neighbour's car, so yours will be nice and tight against the kerb outside your house, further giving credence to that fact you're tucked up between the sheets, sick as a dog and wishing the Imodium would work faster. Man, tummy troubles are the pits!)

As before, gloves. Mustn't forget the gloves.

Your drive is a pleasant one. Sink low in your seat to avoid facial recognition on CCTV. You fancy hiking under the stars, and your neighbour is the perfect companion. After all, you're pally, so spending time with them won't be considered strange. Tell them it's a secret that you're going, no need for anyone else to know. People are so nosy, aren't they, and God, you just want to do something private for once. Hammer that home.

You park up in the middle of nowhere and head off into the woods. Quite the ramble, you're going to have. Off you go, strides steady, chattering away about how Music-Playing Mike gets on your tits and Garage Gary needs telling he can't fix cars out on the street. You're united, have these things in common, and isn't it great?

Your neighbour, well, they don't know they've pissed you off to the point of murder. They soon will, though. Deeper into the woods you go, and they've brought a torch, which is a bit of a bummer because you don't want anyone in passing cars to see the light bobbing around inside the forest, for shit's sake. You suggest they turn it off — "It'll be like being kids, spooked out in the dark. What an adventure!" — and continue on your way until you reach the centre. The trees are thick here, barely any space between the trunks, excellent for what you have in mind. Now, don't mess this bit up. It's crucial you don't frighten the bloody life out of them.

How about this? Let's play hide and seek. Yes, that's it, face the tree, neighbour, and close your eyes. While they're counting to one hundred, I suggest you stomp around a bit to give the impression you've run off. Maybe giggle to begin with — it's all fun and games, isn't it? Take the knife out of your pocket and hold it down by your side. Wait for them to get to ninety-four. That gives you six seconds to creep right up behind them, as silent as you can, and stand there, waiting for them to turn around.

They do, and you plunge that knife into their throat, a stupendous jab that, if your knife is long enough, sees the blade going right through into the bark. Remember, if purchasing such a knife, do so with cash. I can't stress the importance of that enough and do so months in advance of this wickedly wonderful event.

A waitress broke the spell, placing the meal on the table. While eating, Claire thought about getting Andrew into the woods by Shadwell Hill so she could stab the shit out of him, but the idea of spending time with him in a car, not to mention walking amongst creepy trees, brought on a shudder. Okay, *One Hundred Ways to Kill Thy Neighbour* was a joke book, but it'd planted seeds in her mind. Life without Andrew would be so much better. His behaviour had forced her to think this way. She'd never have contemplated bumping someone off until he'd come along. He was *that* annoying.

Of course, she'd never actually do it, but it didn't hurt to dream.

There's a river nearby. Once your neighbour has ceased to exist — party time! — you drag them to the water. In your backpack, you have some rope and plastic carrier bags, and you'll be using them shortly.

For this scenario, we'll say 'dead weight' isn't an issue. I find it's a destruction of happiness to get bogged down with technicalities. You manage to carry your victim to the riverbank and deposit them on the grass. While their soul is on the way to Heaven — or Hell in their case, as they've been such a bloody anvil around your neck these past few months or years — you're busy collecting heavy rocks that just happen to be close by. Fill the bags with them — and we're talking the twenty-pence ones, not the thin, flimsy buggers. You tie the bags up so the handles are bunny ears, then loop rope through them, which is then tied to their wrists and ankles. You might even want to put a couple at their waist for extra sinking assurance, providing there are enough stones.

You're ready to send this bastard to their watery resting place.

Give them a good kick so they roll down the bank and into the water with a beautiful splash. They sink quickly, and you stare in wonder at your magnificent accomplishment. No more pesky neighbour — and isn't that something to celebrate!

The easy part is done. Now you need to go back to their car and put on the protective suit, the shower caps over your shoes, and all but suffocate under the faithful rubber animal mask that smells of new bike tyres. With your CCTV spying stints under your belt, you know how close you can get to home without the vehicle being spotted, but your disguise is extra insurance. You'll leave the car and walk to your house, through the backstreets. Once there, it's imperative you—

"Fancy seeing *you* here, Claire."

Her stomach churned, and the lasagne sat heavy on her tongue. She swallowed. The bastard must have followed her. She'd only been here about twenty minutes, which had given him enough time to sling some clothes on and run after her. Had he been watching from outside the bistro, perving on her while she'd been engrossed in her book?

She glared up at him. "Go away, Andrew."

His forehead crimped, and he cocked his head as though struggling to understand what she'd said. "I'm having the same as you. It looks well nice."

He sat opposite, and she thought about the stones in the carrier bags and how lush the sound of the splash would be if she kicked him into the river. She stood, leaving half of her meal, annoyed he'd encroached on her personal space yet again. What was his problem? He seemed obsessed with her, and his unwanted attention was getting her down.

She shoved her Kindle in her bag and walked out, ignoring his strident call of "Claire? Where are you going?" and his whispered "Skin . . ." that freaked the damn life out of her. What had he said that for?

She'd be early at the Shank but didn't care — anything to get away from him. At least she could ask Rita, the barmaid, to turf him out if he turned up there and bothered her.

Half jogging, she rushed down the street, her heart thudding too fast for her liking. A stitch played up in her side, and she clutched it as if that would make it go away. It didn't. Alone, with no one else around, she felt like crying.

Her vulnerability hit home. No one would see him approach her, what with their curtains being shut, and maybe their TVs would be too loud for them to hear her shouting at him to fuck off and leave her alone. He could do anything to her, and no one would know. Scaring herself silly, she hurried on, thankful when the double doors of the Shank came into view. She pushed through, almost staggering inside in her haste to be with other people.

An overwhelming feeling of relief made her light-headed.

Rita, with her bottle-blonde hair and pink eyeshadow, waved from behind a beer pump. Claire pasted on a smile, going up to the bar on wobbly legs. Her breaths came out shaky, and she told herself off for being so silly. Katy and Viv would be here soon, and she could forget *him* for a while, pretending everything was fine.

Rita finished serving a customer and came over. "What are you having, love?"

"A very large white wine," Claire said, fishing in her bag for her purse.

"Are you all right? You're ever so pale." Rita frowned, reaching below the bar for a glass. She turned side-on and pushed up on the wine optic, the bottles upside down in a glass wall fridge.

"I'm okay, just having problems with my neighbour."

"What are they doing?" Rita placed the full glass in front of Claire.

Handing over a fiver, Claire said, "Oh, it's nothing that can't be fixed. He's just weird and gives me the willies. I'm sure he's been stealing my knickers off the line for months."

"Pardon me? Who the fuck is *that*?" Rita's pencilled-in eyebrows shot up, and she jabbed at the till buttons. "Anyone I know?"

"Andrew Phillips."

"Oh, *him*. The bloke who fancies himself as an actor."

"That's the one." Claire took the change Rita passed her and popped it away.

"Taking your knickers, you say? Have you told the police?"

"Yep, and they can't do a thing about it because I only suspect it's him. The other day, he started mowing his grass in the afternoon and was still doing it by ten at night — with a sodding lamp strapped to his forehead." She went on to tell Rita the lot, relieved to get it off her chest. Speaking to Dad about it when he visited was all well and good, but he wasn't a woman and didn't understand the fear factor that gripped females when men didn't respect boundaries. Katy and Viv just thought it was hilarious, so they didn't help either.

"That's scary, the knicker thing," Rita said. "Hang on, let me just serve that fella there."

While Rita busied herself, Claire looked in the mirror behind the bar, studying each face to make sure Andrew wasn't there. As far as she could tell, he wasn't. Maybe he'd stayed in Bottoms Up after all, feasting on a lasagne. Even him ordering the same food as her was disturbing. Everything about him was.

Katy and Viv breezed in then, all super-tight skinny jeans on ultra-slim frames, wafts of Alien perfume, their blonde air straightened and hanging in perfect sheets. Their wide smiles and big hugs took a lot of Claire's anxiety away. She was safe now, a friend either side of her, the bookends to the bookworm.

Five to eight soon rolled around and, armed with drinks and a few packets of Walkers prawn cocktail, they settled at a table, and Claire wrote their names at the top of the quiz sheet. The jukebox switched off halfway through *Dive* by Ed Sheeran, the punters' chatter seeming loud at first, then dying down as the quiz master tapped the microphone.

The next hour sped by in a frenzy of scribbling answers and agonising over whether they were right. Dakar was the capital of Senegal, she was sure of that, a tomato was a fruit not a vegetable (a nutritionist on the next table argued the toss), but they had no clue who had invented the lawn mower. Claire was confident the rest of their answers were correct, so maybe they had a good shot at winning this week.

With an intermission before the results were revealed, Viv got another round in. The rest of the night went by in a whir of checking their quiz paper, cheering when they'd got one right and booing at the wrong ones. With their papers handed in for verification, it wasn't long, and the quiz master announced the outcome. Once again, Claire's team had lost, and bizarrely, the nutritionist screwed his face up meanly, pumping his fist at them in pleasure. His team had won, despite him fucking it up about tomatoes.

Claire stood, a bit too tipsy, but ho hum, she'd had a nice time. Katy and Viv only lived down the road, so Claire waved them off and headed towards home. She'd walked by herself plenty of times, and it had never bothered her, but tonight, after seeing Andrew, she was a bit unnerved. But it was silly to think he'd still be out at this time, lurking in the darkness. He probably had a dance to practice in his garden and hadn't been able to wait to strip down to his dirty pants after he'd finished his dinner.

She giggled at that, and maybe that was what she ought to do — see the funny side of the situation. He was a sad and annoying little man, nothing more, and if he wanted to keep her knickers, good luck to him.

Claire turned down an alley, a shortcut she usually took when her feet were killing her, like they were tonight. Halfway down, fear came back again, and she cursed herself for taking this route. She ran, her heels rubbing against the inside of her shoes, and wished she hadn't worn them. Out the other end, she blew out a long breath, sweat coating her face from her mad dash. She veered left into the park. Just a short way now, and she'd come out into her street.

A few trees were dotted about, their leafy tops like candy floss on sticks, silhouettes against the dark-grey sky, the moon full and smiling. The halogen lights from the five-a-side footy pitch gave the far-right area a gauzy white glow. Someone was out that way, the diamond-wire fence surrounding the pitch a backdrop to a slender, black-infused figure who appeared to have their hands in their pockets, probably some bloke who'd finished a match with his mates.

They darted forward, running full pelt towards her, and it took Claire a moment to realise what was going on: she was in a park, alone with someone else, a stranger, and they headed her way. Her feet refused to obey for a second, but then she was off, legging it to towards the opening between the hedges that led to her street. She ran fast, high heels digging into the grass, one of them sticking. Her foot came out of it, and she bolted forward, the momentum sending her sprawling, the ground cold and damp beneath her knees and palms.

She glanced to where the person was, but they were gone. Spooked beyond belief, she left her shoe where it was, too intent on getting to safety to give much of a toss about it. At a lopsided trot, she made it to the hedges, fright sending her breathless, her eyes stinging, and she berated herself for walking home, for not getting a taxi. You read about women going missing all the time. Just recently it had been on the news. Some poor love called Helen hadn't been seen since last week. And here Claire was, flirting with danger, just asking for someone to abduct her.

"Skin . . ."

The voice came from nowhere and everywhere, raspy and whiny, echoing inside her head. Claire's legs almost went from under her, and she barked out an incoherent shout, launching herself between the hedges and into her street. Adrenaline fuelling her, she staggered along the pavement, grit digging into her bare foot. Her house seemed too far away, and she was sure someone was breathing behind her. Other footsteps matched her pace, and she risked a glance over her shoulder. The figure from the park followed, hood low over their face, hands plunged into the front pockets of their sweatshirt.

"Fuck, fuck, fuck," she whispered, facing ahead and running as best she could.

Her front door had never looked so good. There it was, only a few paces, her garden path calling out for her to hurry, hurry, hurry, and she pushed on, nearly at her gate now.

The blow took her breath away, the back of her head pounding from the force, and she opened her mouth to scream, but nothing came out, terror snatching her voice and holding it in a tight fist. She fell to the pavement, rolling onto her side, clutching her skull.

Wet on her hands. Warmth. Liquid.

Blood.

Panicking, she struggled to stand, grabbing her low garden wall to steady herself. She caught sight of whoever had hit her, to her left, coming closer, no face visible, the streetlight behind them ensuring shadows shrouded the features.

"Skin," they whispered.

And she knew — it was him. Knew she had the proof for the police to do something about him now, except he was dragging her back down the street, to the park. She managed to let out another shout, then a gloved hand clamped over her mouth, and she had the chilling thought that the police wouldn't be able to do a damn thing about *this* either.

CHAPTER SIX

Fran and Leona had gone home at ten p.m., but Bethany and Mike had agreed to stay on until midnight. There were a few things left to do before she could rest easy.

Leona had been through CCTV regarding the woods, and while most of the car owners had been contacted and cleared, three had indistinct number plates, either shadows falling across them or dirt obscuring the info. Frustrating to say the least, but there was nothing they could do about it. One of those three people could be their killer — or even one of the ones with alibis. A good liar could fool anyone if they tried hard enough.

"Do you know," she said to Mike, leaning back in Fran's chair, "the number of times we've been lied to over the years, and it turned out the people who lied actually 'did it' . . . Does that reflect on us? I mean, are we losing our touch or what?"

He glanced away from his monitor to look over at her. "Nah, just means they're getting clever. If they watch the same crime shows I do, they'll be getting savvy in how to fool us. Why?"

"No reason. Was just thinking."

Wondering if I'm not instinctually picking up on things these days.

Facebook had thrown up the usual — selfies, memes, recipes, stuff like that. Helen had minimal friends, and she'd been tagged a lot by Rose Harding who was either posing with elephants in the background or in a car with a monkey peering through the windscreen, cheesy grin in place. To put it bluntly, fuck all the team could get their teeth into. Messenger hadn't thrown up anything of importance either — Fran had cracked the password for both sites: tipsandtalonsrule.

As for sales of Victorian dresses, boots and that little velvet bag, emails had gone out to all sellers on Amazon, eBay, Etsy and other online stores to see if anyone was willing to divulge if they'd sent goods to Shadwell and the surrounding areas. With data protection a high priority for vendors these days, Bethany didn't hold out any hope of getting an actual name and address, but if someone responded that a sale of those items had been made, Kribbs could sort the paperwork to receive the vital information — she prayed it would send them straight to the killer's door.

Chance would be a fine thing. Something will fuck it up.

Tomorrow, Bethany and Mike planned to interview the boss and employees at Tips and Talons, and also the family friend who was supposed to have had her nails done by Helen. Mike had phoned Fay Chown earlier and got the name and address.

Now, Bethany pored over the crime scene photos Isabelle had sent her, enlarging them on Fran's monitor, desperate to find something the human eye had missed while they'd been in the woods. Dinner, a fish-and-chip takeaway, had long ago been sloshed down with cans of Pepsi, and having consumed exorbitant amounts of coffee since then, Bethany was buzzing, not to mention needing a wee.

Mike was at the end of another CCTV trawl, searching for vehicles that had been at or around Potter's Yard last Sunday night.

"Ay up," he said. "Would you say this is the same car noted as being by the woods — one of the ones with an unclear number plate?"

Bethany got up and walked over to his desk. He had two windows up on screen, side by side, the grainy images of cars on each, both shots at nighttime. The shape was the same, and because of the pictures being black and white, it was hard to tell if they were identical in colour, but they were certainly in a similar shade bracket.

"Could be," she said.

Her phone went off in her pocket, so she took it out. It could only be work this late. Wasn't like she had any friends who'd want to chat, was it? Vinny and Mike were all she had, and Vinny only appeared in dreams and spoke in her head.

The name on the screen confirmed it. Ursula Fringwell, the nighttime desk sergeant.

Bethany swiped the screen. "Yep."

"Um, probably not for you, but seeing as a missing person ended up as one of your cases, I thought I'd give you a bell anyway. Nicola Eccles went to a callout where someone reported hearing a female shouting in their street around an hour ago — around tenish. They went outside, and there's a handprint on someone's wall — blood."

"How the hell did they spot that on brick in the dark?"

"It's one of those ones with a shelf thing on top. A ledge, maybe so you can put plant pots on it, and it's light-grey stone."

"Ah, I see. So why do you think this is something for us?"

"The woman who lives in the house with the handprint isn't answering, and she's blonde, like Helen Chown. I've run the resident's name, and she's down as having made complaints about her next-door neighbour, an Andrew Phillips, who also is not answering. She'd rung us about a few things: him stealing her knickers off the washing line, climbing over her fence into her back garden and engaging in unwanted conversation, and generally appearing in places she goes — so, a stalker vibe going on. He's been asked to leave her alone and stop walking about in the street in his underpants by . . . Glen and Tory, on two occasions."

"You what?"

"Hmm. It bothered me enough to ring you."

"Okay, well, seeing as we're here, we'll go, but it probably isn't anything for us to deal with."

"Here's the kicker. Someone saw her being dragged down the street into the park."

"Ah, then that's a different story. Abduction, we'll take."

"Penny Dickens is partnering Nicola tonight, and she went into the park. Torch beam picked up a shoe stuck in the grass by the heel."

"Okay, right, we'll get down there now. Where is it?"

"The woman potentially abducted is a Claire Ellis at sixty-seven Vampton Road, and the park's the one behind the houses."

"Ta. Write that on a Post-it for me, will you? We'll collect it on our way out." She shoved her phone away. "We've got a job, matey."

"Thought so." Mike took screenshots of the CCTV captures and saved them, then scribbled down the times the cars had been spotted and on which file. He closed the browser windows and shut down his computer.

Bethany did the same with Fran's, and she messaged Isabelle to warn her she might be needed in a bit, depending on what Bethany and Mike found. Then they were off, collecting the Post-it from Ursula and driving to Vampton Road.

The street was more like an avenue, really, the pavements either side bordered by intermittent trees, birches by the look of the white trunks with large black speckles. Wheelie bins stood on the grass between the paths and the road, collection tomorrow, most likely. Cars sat bumper to bumper, the homes not having driveways, just gardens separated from the street by brick walls topped with the ledges Ursula had mentioned.

The police car parked adjacent to a resident's narrowed the throughway into one lane, so Bethany eased up behind it. Nicola or Penny had acted on the safe side and cordoned off the area outside Claire Ellis' house, and farther down, crime scene tape flickered in the breeze, draped between two hedges. The park entrance was probably there then. Penny stood in front, hands behind her back, hi-vis coat dull beneath an amber streetlamp, which had turned it korma-coloured.

Bethany and Mike got out.

"I'll go and speak to Penny," Mike said. "See what's what with her."

Bethany nodded and approached Nicola, who walked down a path after speaking to a neighbour. Nicola took out her notebook, and together they moved to stand beneath one of the trees for a bit of privacy.

"What have you got?" Bethany asked quietly, conscious of earwiggers — some of the bedroom windows were open close by, and a few people had their noses pressed to the glass.

Nicola related what Ursula had told Bethany. "Since then, I've managed to speak to a few neighbours. Oh, before I forget, we're waiting for Glen — he went off shift but has come back on as I think we need someone at the other park entrance. Penny also spotted a piece of material snagged on the hedge, on the park side, like someone's clothing caught and ripped off."

"Okay. The neighbours?"

"The one who heard the shout and found the blood — he's in sixty-two." Nicola handed over her notebook so Bethany could read it. "More blood is on the pavement by Ellis' house — drips, I assume from a fresh wound. I've popped an evidence marker there."

Bethany finished reading. "Has anyone else said anything?"

Nicola nodded and flipped a page over. "The neighbour directly next door in sixty-eight isn't answering, but the one on the other side at sixty-six, a Ginny Mansell, said Ellis has been having problems with sixty-eight. Someone called Andrew Phillips. Mansell said she's heard Ellis telling Phillips to get out of her garden on numerous occasions, and he has a habit of being outside in his underpants."

"I heard he does that. Phillips has had warnings to leave her alone and to dress appropriately in public."

"The underpants are apparently always dirty." Nicola screwed her face up.

"God, he sounds like he needs to know what Surf is for. A bit of Vanish as well while he's at it." *Why would anyone want to walk about with filthy pants on? In front of people?* She shook her head, mind officially boggled.

"Mansell also said she tried ringing Ellis just before we arrived. She was worried after seeing the blood on the wall. No answer. I have Ellis' number here."

Bethany wrote it down. "Okay, well, I don't think I'll speak to the neighbours again, you've done a good job there. I saw on your notes there are a few people not answering — what it must be like to be a sound sleeper, eh? I think I'll get Isabelle down here — better safe than sorry. You carry on doing door-to-door. Thanks."

Bethany walked to Mike. "I'll just message Isabelle and ask her to bring a few officers with her. The park ought to be searched."

They ducked under the tape between the hedges and entered the park. Penlights out, they carefully picked their way across the field, taking their time. Bethany spied nothing in the grass until they happened upon the shoe and the evidence marker beside it. The heel was indeed wedged into the ground, and a circle of blood marred the inside where a blister must have formed on the wearer's foot — a handy sample of DNA to match with the blood outside Claire Ellis'. With this looking more sinister by the minute, Bethany made a decision: when Isabelle and her team arrived, they'd use the ram on Claire's front door and enter the property.

Another torch beam flashed down at the other park entrance, to the right, flickering with their station's version of Morse code: *Person in blue here*. So Glen had arrived. Good. She flashed back.

"There's material snagged on the hedge," Mike said. "Penny said about it."

"Okay, we'll have a look now."

In the park entrance, Bethany shone her light on the hedge. Yes, black sparkly material, about an inch square, clung to a small protruding branch. It shivered slightly in the breeze.

"Hang on," Mike said. "See that?" He pointed next to the fabric.

Hair. Blonde. Long.

"Abduction," he said.

"I agree. Let's get back to the street. I want to knock and see if that Andrew Phillips bloke is in."

They dipped beneath the scene tape again.

"Penny, can you let SOCO know when they come this way that there's also blonde hair by the material." Bethany glanced up the way. "Actually, I'll tell them myself."

Isabelle and her team had arrived, the vans hogging the majority of the road width behind Bethany's car. An officer was already at work taking pictures of the wall while another waited nearby with a swab to take a blood sample. A third officer was on his hands and knees in Claire's front garden, while Isabelle spoke to the rest of her colleagues by one of the vans.

Bethany strode up to her. "Sorry to interrupt. State of play is we *have* to get into number sixty-seven, plus people are needed in the park." She explained about the shoe, hair and material.

"I'll send my guys in now," Isabelle said.

She issued orders, and her team got to work.

"We need to get hold of her immediate neighbour." Bethany filled her in about Andrew Phillips. "Weirdo, by the sounds of it."

"Dirty pants?" Isabelle whispered.

"I know. There's nowt so queer as folk."

She gestured to Mike and they nipped up Andrew Phillips' path, Bethany knocking on the door. She didn't expect an answer so was surprised when the door swung open and a slim man in his late-thirties/early forties stood there in manky Y-fronts, his pale skin on full display.

"Andrew Phillips?" Bethany asked, showing her ID and stating their names.

He blinked as though he'd just woken up. "Yes . . . What's going on out here?" He gazed at the activity, his Adam's apple bobbing. His eyes widened at officers banging at Claire's door with a ram. "Did she get locked in or something?"

Bethany ignored that. "Where have you been this evening?"

"Um . . . Let me think." He rubbed his eyebrow, staring at SOCOs filing into Claire's. "Err, Bottoms Up Bistro. I had my dinner there. Claire will tell you, as she was there an' all."

"What did you eat?" She wanted to see if his answer was immediate or if he had to think of a meal because he hadn't actually eaten one.

"Lasagne, chips, and salad. Very nice, too, although Claire left half of hers."

Was this one of his stalking episodes, or had he truly gone there with her? The latter didn't ring true if she'd complained to the police about him. Why would you want to have dinner with someone who upset you?

"Did you eat with Miss Ellis then?" she asked.

"No, she was just there when I went in. I sat at the table with her, but she got up and walked out."

"Did she say why?"

"No. She told me to go away at first, though."

"And why would she do that?"

"I don't know. I've been trying to work it out all night."

He appeared genuinely perplexed. Maybe he was one of those people who didn't understand personal space or social cues that let him know when to back off.

"Where did you go after Bottoms Up?"

"I went for a walk. There was this man with his dog, a little thing, a Jack Russell. We talked for ages. It's Mr Lutworth. Lives at number seven. Then I kicked a ball about for a bit on the five-a-side pitch — there was one lying about from a match, so I used it."

"By yourself? And where's that?"

"In the park back there." He jerked his thumb inside his house. "And yep, by myself."

"How long did you stay out there for?"

"Dunno, but I got home about nine, half nine."

"Did you see anyone else there?"

"Only the football players. There were a group of men leaving as I arrived."

"Did anyone see you come home?"

He shrugged. "Maybe Ginny. She's always nosing. Ask her?"

"We will. We'll also go and see Mr Lutworth, plus find out who the men were at the pitch."

No facial reaction whatsoever from him. She'd wanted some kind of tell, like a tic or a darkening of his eyes to tell her he'd been up to no good, but he didn't look guilty at all.

He shrugged again. "Claire's going to be upset you broke her door. She's very proud of her house."

"Do you know Claire well?"

"We talk a lot. Well, she listens while I tell her things. She's nice."

"Did you see her after being at Bottoms Up?"

"No, but I'd say she went to quiz night at the Shank. She always does quiz night."

He sounded a sandwich short, but was he anyone to worry about? His weedy frame . . . well, he didn't seem sturdy enough to drag someone down the street. Still, he might be strong regardless, so she'd keep an open mind. For now, she'd leave him be, except . . . maybe she'd test him.

"Would you mind if we have a look around your house?" she asked.

He stepped back. "Be my guest."

No hesitation. That's in his favour.

Mike went inside.

"Claire likes reading on her Kindle," Andrew said, scratching his arse. "And she has lots of different handbags. Loads of colours. They get delivered by the Asian driver."

"You seem to know a lot about her." Bethany frowned. "Is that because you watch her?"

"No. From talking. We just talk. That's all we do. She doesn't like my pants. She hasn't said so, but I know these things."

"I'm aware of the complaints she made against you. What do you have to say about that?"

"She doesn't like being friendly. I just want to be friends."

"You should respect her desire *not* to be. What's all this about stealing her knickers?"

"Not me!" He stuck his bottom lip out. Sulking?

A creak sounded from inside, then a sliding clatter.

"What's he doing in my loft?" Andrew asked. "Nothing up there but fluff. That yellow fluff."

"You said it was fine to check your house," Bethany said. "That's what my colleague is doing."

"What are you looking for?" He tilted his head and ran his palms down his hairless chest.

Might as well be honest. "To see if Claire's in there."

"She wouldn't come inside my house. She has her own."

Mike came down the stairs and out onto the path shaking his head. *She isn't in there.*

"Okay, Mr Phillips." Bethany smiled. "We need to get on now. Thanks for your time."

She walked down his path and to her car, where she and Mike suited up. They entered Claire's whilst Andrew remained on his doorstep, a questionable stain on the side of his pants. Bethany shuddered with revulsion and made a note to check whether Phillips was under a mental healthcare team. He didn't seem right, and she didn't want to peck at him over the coming days if he had issues that she needed to be aware of. He might have just got fixated with Claire and didn't mean her any harm. While that must be incredibly uncomfortable for Claire, Andrew might need to be treated gently and have it explained that he couldn't just force his need for friendship on someone.

In the hallway, she sent Ursula a message.

Bethany: CAN YOU ASK SOMEONE TO DELVE INTO ANDREW PHILLIPS, SIXTY-EIGHT VAMPTON, SPECIFICALLY FOR MENTAL HEALTH. ALSO TO HAVE A LOOK AT CCTV

OF THE AREA AROUND VAMPTON. I NEED TO KNOW WHO BOOKED THE FIVE-A-SIDE PITCH TONIGHT. LET ME KNOW WHEN YOU FIND ANYTHING OUT. I HAVE A MOBILE NUMBER FOR YOU TO CHECK. IF YOU CAN, SEE WHICH TOWER IT LAST PINGED — I REALISE THAT MIGHT NOT GET DONE UNTIL THE MORNING.

She added Claire's number.

Ursula: OKIE DOKIE.

Then she moved back to the front door and called Nicola, who was over the road peering at the grass verge. Nicola ran up Claire's path.

Bethany whispered in her ear, because Andrew was still close by, "Go and speak to a Mr Lutworth at number seven. That bloke right here claims to have spoken to him tonight. I want a specific time."

Nicola nodded and walked away.

Bethany turned and smiled at Mike, closing the door to. She gestured with her head for them to move farther into the house. In the kitchen at the back, while two SOCOs checked cupboards, she said, "What the hell did you make of Phillips?"

"Not right upstairs." Mike tapped his temple. "But he didn't look dodgy to me at all."

"Hmm. I'm not sure . . ." Was she grasping at it being him because of what she'd thought earlier about them losing their touch?

Mike scratched his nose with his wrist. "If people say they saw him where he said he was . . ."

"I know, but what about after half nine? The shout was reported about ten. Nicola and Penny came straight away. How did he get Claire through the park, to wherever he took her, then back indoors without them seeing him?"

"It's possible, *if* it was him, that he could have got in round the back. Neighbours would have been too busy nosing out the front."

"Fair enough. With Claire reporting him to us, we can't discount the fact he upset her enough for her to ring the police. Someone like that sits at the top of our list."

"We'll look into him."

She nodded, and they toured the house, Bethany dead on her feet.

CHAPTER SEVEN

Andrew closed his front door and streaked around the house, checking whether that policeman had disturbed anything. More to the point, whether he'd found the silhouette body map where Andrew had hidden it in a cylindrical poster tube down the back of the fridge freezer. There it was, a carrier bag of stolen knickers on top.

His things were safe and sound.

Hopefully, the woman copper, Smith, had bought his behaviour, thinking it was his normal way. He was an actor after all. Playing an imbecile hadn't been too difficult. Stacey Maxey would have been so proud of his performance.

Or maybe not, considering . . .

It had been a bloody close call, though, getting home without being seen. Earlier, once he'd known for certain he'd steal Claire, when she'd brushed him off one time too many in Bottoms Up — *How dare you!* — he'd put the stolen Ford with the doctored plates in the car park beside the five-a-side footballers' vehicles. Later, once the Ford sat there alone, he'd snatched her from the street and took her to the boot, stuffing her inside. He'd gagged her, smacked her on the head twice with a monkey wrench until she'd blacked out, then shut her inside. He'd raced home, vaulting the rear fence and entering his house the back way. While that uniform copper had been knocking, he'd been securing the map and underwear, then, a bit later, those other two had knocked, and he'd successfully pulled it off that they'd woken him up. *And* that he was a weirdo.

The question was, how would he get back out there to drive Claire to his secret location? She could wake up at any time, kick at the boot, and the police nosing about in the park might hear her if they were checking that way.

Fucking hell.

He was annoyed and jittery because things hadn't gone to plan. Someone must have heard Claire shout or seen him with her and called the police. He moved to the spare room window at the back and peered between a slit in the curtains where they didn't quite meet in the middle. A big torch had been set up in the park, and it only illuminated the area where Claire had lost her shoe, the clumsy girl, leaving the outside edges in darkness. That was what had cost him, got them seeing the park as a place of interest, that fucking shoe. Thankfully, the halogen by the pitch only came on if you stood too close to the diamond-wire fence — he'd learnt that while waiting for Claire to walk through the park. Where he'd left the car was outside the sensor zone.

He'd give it half an hour then chance it. He could climb over his fence and stay close to the perimeter of the park, sidling round until he reached the Ford. He'd push the car onto the street. If he kept the headlights off until he got out on the road, by the time the coppers heard anything, he'd be long gone.

But what if the officers knocked at his door again and he didn't answer?

Shit. What a dilemma.

* * *

Claire stifled a whimper upon waking. She shook, cold and afraid in the boot of that car the man had thrown her into.

Not the man. Andrew.

It was moving, although the engine wasn't on. The sound of grit under the tyres loud, she was jostled a little as the vehicle went over a dip, then moved faster, as if going down an incline. A jolt, a door slamming, the engine turning over. From the way gravity pulled her to one side, she'd say they'd gone round a corner. And another.

She kicked the interior and pummelled it with her fists, and fuck, her head hurt where he'd hit her in the street and from the two cracks he'd rained down on her when he'd dumped her in the boot. She tried shoving her foot into the panel that encased the lights so she could break them. Anyone following might think it was dodgy and report it, but the fucking thing wouldn't budge.

A long stretch — or it seemed long — of continual driving, then another few turns. She'd never been out this way so had no idea where he was taking her. He'd marched her to the five-a-side car park, and she knew there was an access road beside it that led to the other side of the estate, but after that?

She continued whacking the boot.

Please let someone hear me.

The gag muffled her screams — screams of desperation and terror.

She remembered her top had ripped on the hedge, and her hair had gotten tangled in it, tugging at the roots, bringing burning pain. He hadn't cared, just ripped her off the branches and lunged across the field, her scalp throbbing. She'd tried to dig her remaining high heel into the grass, to leave divots and a trail that someone might follow once they knew she was missing, but the way he'd carried her along, she hadn't found purchase. Would the divots be seen amongst the grass, though? She'd managed to kick her shoe off, but he'd spotted her attempt at leaving a clue — a second one, seeing as her other stiletto was out there somewhere. He'd scooped it up and put it in the boot with her.

She stopped hammering and brushed her fingertips over her top as far as she could reach . . . and found a hole. Something clung to it, probably leaves, a cruel reminder of how close to home she'd once been. She checked her body, patting herself down, and a twig or something had got snagged in her hair.

Why had he taken her? And where were they going?

A short while later, her throat hoarse from more screams, the engine's rumble died down, and the car slowed, coming to a complete stop. A second jostle, the door opening then closing, the boot lid lifting, revealing darkness and an even darker silhouette.

Andrew.

She shouted at him, but the words weren't recognisable with her mouth full. "You mad fucking wanker!"

"Oh, shut up, Claire."

Oh yes, it was definitely him. She'd recognise that whine anywhere. Christ Almighty, she was so angry now. All her fear had vanished with the rise of her temper and her need to lash out at him. Who the hell did he think he was? He'd been pissing her off for ages, months, and now he'd decided to kidnap her?

She sat up and played dumb until she was out of the car and on solid ground. Then she could check where she was and work out the best course of action. She stared at him, blinking, as her handbag moved beside her — thank God she always had the strap going across her body in case someone tried to steal it. Her being conscientious meant she hadn't lost it. She kept a Sharpie in there after seeing on YouTube that it wasn't classed as a weapon and you could do a lot of damage with it, especially in the soft part of the neck. If only she could get to it . . .

He grabbed the tops of her arms, his fingertips and nails digging in, and yanked her out of the car. How was he so strong when he was so weedy? She didn't kick or try to hit him. Didn't say a word. Didn't run. Not until she knew what was what. He spun her around, gripping her wrists behind her back, and she took in her surroundings.

The bright moon with its wide smile and arched eyebrows, puffy clouds for hair and a long beard.

A courtyard of some kind, with rough concrete. Like a driveway.

A building — old, abandoned, just like in the books she read, and God, she was well and truly fucked if this went the way of a thriller.

He pushed her forward. She stumbled, then righted herself.

Trees, in the very far distance, houses close by them, tiny boxes of blackness spotted with miniscule light-filled squares where people lived and breathed an evening without fear seeping into their marrow.

Small stones beneath her bare feet.

The extremely faint hum of traffic, perhaps from an A road somewhere. Each vehicle made a *swoosh, swoosh* sound as it drove along. People were in their safe existences, with nothing more to worry about than making the rent payment on time or buying little Davey his next pair of shoes.

A door. Wooden. Ancient. Him inserting a key — he owned this place?

He threw the door wide and shoved her in, taking her to the back. The smell of must and damp hit her, dust motes dancing in the light of the moon coming through a smeared window.

A corner in an empty room. Her standing in it, his hands on her shoulders, pressing her down to the floor, so cold on her backside.

He let her wrists go and stepped away. Half of him, visible via Luna, showed he had the same hoodie on as earlier when he'd chased her through the park. And gloves. Black leather. Murderer's gloves.

Where had he been between then and driving her away?

"If you don't do what I want, you'll find out how skin burns, Claire Bear."

Don't call me that. Don't you ever call me that.

That was Dad's name for her. Only him.

Oh God, Dad's going to be so upset.

And what did Andrew mean? Was he going to *burn* her?

She shook her head, frantic now, panic setting up a flutter of wings in her belly and chest. Thinking of Dad had done that. Slowly, careful not to draw Andrew's attention to her hand, she slid it inside her bag, praying she didn't disturb anything enough to mean things clanked against each other. A lipstick on her Kindle, her compact mirror on her phone case.

She felt around, barely moving.

"A woman once told me skin is the closest thing to us, and to have someone else's on ours is an honour." He let out a long breath. "Will you let your skin touch mine?"

The thought of it revolted her. She suppressed a heave. Found the Sharpie. Curled her fingers around it. Held it in such a way that she could stab him.

"What are you doing?" he asked. Head tilt.

She hated it when he did that.

"Nothing," she said, but it came out as just a sound behind the gag.

He moved forward and took the material away, dropping it to the floor. Her mouth was so bloody dry. She swallowed, and it created a noise, a crackle, probably only inside her head. She gently pulled the Sharpie out, staring into his eyes to keep his attention on her face — his features were clear now, the moon-glow through the glass in the back door bright.

"You're mine," he said.

I'm no one's.

"You'll be close to me."

I'll be far away. Inside my head.

"You'll love me."

Knob. Off.

She rammed the Sharpie up, towards his neck, but his hand shot out and caught her wrist. Clamping. Squeezing. Pinching. Teeth gritted. An animalistic sound wrenching from him. Angry. He was so . . . fucking . . . angry.

Oh God . . .

"Did you think I wouldn't know you were up to something?" he asked, his grin wide. "Silly girl."

She kicked, her foot connecting with his shin. Tried higher to get to his groin, but from her position, she was too scrunched up and him too close. He punched her in the stomach with his free hand — *That hurts so much!* — and she dipped her chin to her chest, snapping her eyes shut to concentrate on not letting him hear any cry of pain. She stuffed it down, determined not to show weakness.

He wrenched her upright, her wrist killing her from his tight grip, and took her bag off her, throwing it behind him.

Such a strange thing to think at a time like this but: *My Kindle might break . . .*

"If you're a good girl, I'll let you read your books while you're here." He snatched the Sharpie and lobbed it across the room.

While I'm here. Does that mean he's going to let me go? Take me somewhere else?

"I'll have to buy you a charger, unless you have one in your bag."

She wished she had a Kindle that connected to the internet. She could have logged on to Facebook, got one of the girls in Books & Bags to send for help. Melanie Atkins and Kay Hutcherson would ring the police, no questions asked.

Shit.

He pushed her, and she sailed back down, landing on her arse, her tailbone throbbing.

She was going to kill him if it was the last thing she did.

* * *

With her being naked, her wrists and ankles tied, Andrew reckoned Claire looked like a plucked chicken, ready to be roasted. He laughed at that — roasted — and she gave him a filthy look. As well she might. He'd secured her to the radiator pipe.

He'd already spent far too much time here with her, and that annoyed him. She could get him in such trouble.

"I have to go," he said. "You have your books, so be grateful. Think about skin while I'm gone, Claire Bear.

Think about yours on mine. If you don't say yes to that, I'll just take it."

She frowned, probably wondering how he'd 'take' her skin.

If she didn't behave, she'd find out.

"I'll be back at some point." Best to be vague.

He left her there, where she'd get cold and uncomfortable, her hair growing greasier by the day, her body smelling, stomach calling out for food, mouth desperate for water. She'd be glad of a wash when he offered it to her, glad to agree to their skin touching. And if she didn't allow that?

Well, he'd just have to burn her.

* * *

Claire couldn't stand the loneliness anymore — or the shit going around in her head. She'd thought of everything she could in order to get out of this, but with Andrew gone, she couldn't even persuade him to set her free. She gave in and, with only fifty percent battery left on her Kindle, switched it on, plunging herself into a world where she might just find the right tip to help her out of this mess.

SCENARIO SIXTEEN

Necessity: You must have a strong stomach.

ITEMS NEEDED:
AXE
PLASTIC SHEETING
MEAT GRINDER
SLEEPING PILLS
CUSHION

Let's play at being Dexter, shall we? You know the TV series, yes? If you're not familiar, he tends to find a suitable kill location and dresses the room up with plastic sheeting. That way, blood is contained. And there will be a lot of blood.

We'll assume you have a garage or a spare room. Ensure your plastic is in place, overlapping so there are no gaps. It would be handy to have a large metal drum. You can use this to burn the plastic in later. Alternatively, you could bury it in a remote location. Whatever. Like I said before . . . technicalities. They're boring.

For this fantasy kill, everything will go smoothly. You've invited your neighbour to yours for a meal. Ensure they come in via the back of your house — tell them Bossy Bert has been getting on your wick and you don't want him knowing who you have round at your place. Once the meal has been consumed, offer them a drink, which you will add an ingredient to. You should have previously either ground up some sleeping pills using a pestle and mortar (there's a nice grey marble one on Amazon, £19.99. Beautiful, darling!) or open up the tablet casing and tip the powder out. Use four, just to be sure your victim drops off nicely, hopefully banging their face on your dining table so you can laugh your head off about it.

It isn't rocket science to get hold of such medication, by the way. GPs are good for that sort of thing. Have a good old moan about how you've got insomnia. Oh, the hours you're kept awake! That should do the trick, and a prescription will be produced. Amazing.

Once they are soundly snoozing, drag their sorry arse into your garage/spare room/chosen place of doom.

Undress them. I know, I know, it might not be pleasant, but needs must.

Smother them with the cushion. That's it, right over their nose and mouth. A couple of minutes of pressing down hard should kill them. It would be longer if they weren't drugged, just so you know for future reference. And this way, they're so out of it, you won't have the inconvenience of them thrashing about. Always a bargain, that.

Go and do some washing up. Clear the table. Perhaps hoover if you have a mind. This will ensure enough time passes for the blood to coagulate a little — not so much mess, then, you see. I advise an hour, no more. As your next job might take a while, depending on your strength and dexterity with an axe, you need to get a move on here. Rigor mortis waits for no man.

Return to the garage.

Pick up the axe.

And have a murder party with it.

Once your neighbour is chopped into as many pieces as you can manage, use a lovely sharp knife to cut the flesh away from the bones. This flesh can then be placed in your meat grinder. If you're brave, you'll use the mince for an extra-special Bolognese or chilli. Perhaps you'll feed it to another neighbour who gets your goat. Make meat parcels, wrap them in clingfilm, and pop them in your freezer. If you don't wish to eat your neighbour, the frozen packages will make transporting to a disposal site easier, plus, there'll be no seeping blood.

Bonus!

Of course, when handling the clingfilm and meat, what do you need to do?

That's it! Wear gloves.

Claire couldn't see for tiredness, could no longer concentrate on the words. Much as she didn't want to sleep, her eyes weren't complying with her order for them to stay open. Reading at night always sent her into the abyss. She turned the Kindle off and placed it beside her.

When was he going to come back? Part of her wanted him to so she could try the next tack, be nice to him and let their skin touch. If that was all he wanted, she'd comply, no matter how much it sickened her. But the other part of her . . . No, she didn't want him anywhere near her. Didn't want to see him, hear his nasal breathing, his stupid little voice . . .

Before she'd picked up her Kindle, Claire had tried to free herself from the radiator pipe. The knots in the rope were too tight, though. She'd even manoeuvred so she could bite it, gnaw the knot loose that way, but it hadn't worked.

She'd try again in a bit. Even if she only managed to undo the rope on the pipe, she could hop to the door and attempt to escape.

She shouted for the umpteenth time — bloody useless when they were in the middle of nowhere, but the survival instinct was strong. Her throat was sore, her mouth arid, and she'd already wet herself, the liquid still beneath her arse, a puddle on the bare concrete floor.

Skin.

She remembered him saying it in the garden. In the park. In their street.

Why was he so obsessed with it?

She tipped her head back against the wall and closed her eyes.

Just for a minute. It wouldn't hurt.

* * *

He'd made it home without detection. The police in their white suits were too far away to notice him in the shadows, too busy inspecting the grass, doing their jobs. They'd appeared tiny from where he'd been walking around the perimeter. His heart pounded hard, though, from the adrenaline rush, giving him a bit of gyp.

He stripped down to his underpants, so comfortable this way. Clothes, unless they were the ones he put on for plays, suffocated his skin.

Andrew thought about getting the silhouette map out, putting it back where it belonged, then decided against it. He'd wait until the police had gone from the street.

Glass in hand, he pressed it to the wall and listened to them moving about inside Claire's. They must be checking it thoroughly to still be there.

"Absolutely sod all," a woman said, sounding far away.

Of course there would be sod all. He hadn't been into Claire's house to leave anything behind.

Not like at Helen's.

CHAPTER EIGHT

Stacey had found out he'd stolen her skin. The skin she'd burnt while she'd been sunning herself in Tenerife. The stupid caretaker must have been watching him through the glass window in the rehearsal room door. Stacey wasn't happy. Had even gone so far as to say if he ever did anything so bizarre again, she'd kick him off the troupe, the cheeky bitch.

She'd reminded him of that woman, *and all the years of keeping his rage inside had spilt out. He was ready to begin again.*

He waited now, beside the community centre, where the bins stood shoulder to shoulder down the alley. She'd be out soon, waltzing along here, and he'd follow her to where she always parked in the quiet road behind — a road with fields opposite, no one around to see a thing.

The creak of the centre door opening had him pressing his back to the wall, seeping farther into the darkness that was his current best friend. She appeared, head bent, attention on her phone, the light from the screen glowing on her face. She smiled — whatever she read was amusing.

He'd have a look at any private messages later, see what was so funny.

Stacey was passing him now, so beautifully unaware he was . . . right . . . there. He followed her on silent feet. Waited until she almost got to the other end of the alley and—

Fuck! What a rush!

—whacked her on the top of her head with an iron bar.

Down she went, out of it.

In the boot next.

He took her keys and phone, jumped in the driver's seat, and pulled away, gloves snug on his hands. Arriving at the secret place, he carried her inside and dumped her in the corner. Undressed her. Tied her up and attached her to the radiator pipe. She came round, eyes still closed, groaning, groggy, blood dripping down her face from the gash on her scalp, and he crouched, leaning forward, his nose nearly touching hers.

She opened her eyes, registered him, and screamed.

The punch to her cheek shut her up.

"Now then, Miss Maxey, you're going to give me more of that skin."

He stood, walked backwards to an old wooden crate in the far corner. His heat tool, the battery already charged, sat patiently waiting. Her eyes widened when he switched it on and the blue flame sped out.

"I'll burn you just enough for the skin to peel in a few days."

The trouble was, he got too close a couple of times, and the hotness gnawed into her, blisters forming.

He'd get it right eventually.

Everyone had to start somewhere, didn't they.

She screamed until no sound came out, on and on, mouth wide, in silent torture.

It got on his nerves, so he burnt her big fat gob an' all.

Her phone bleeped, and he switched the fire tool off, placing it in its holder so it didn't singe the crate. A message bar sat on her screen, with the option for him to read or reply.

He clicked READ and scrolled back to the start of the convo.

Stacey: YOU KNOW THE WEIRDO BLOKE IN THE PLAY? YOU'LL NEVER GUESS WHAT . . . HE STOLE MY SUNBURN PEEL!!!

Helen: EH? I DON'T GET IT. HOW DID HE EVEN . . .

Stacey: OKAY, I WAS BEING GROSS AND PICKING IT OFF THE OTHER NIGHT, YOU

KNOW WHAT I'M LIKE. HE APPARENTLY SCOOPED IT UP IN A PIECE OF PAPER AND TOOK IT.

Helen: OMG, WHAT A BLOODY CREEPY BASTARD!

Stacey: I KNOW! AND TO THINK I FELT SORRY FOR HIM. I MEAN, HE SMELLS.

Helen: EWW. GET RID OF HIM.

Stacey: I PLAN TO — RIGHT AFTER THIS PLAY. IT'S TOO LATE IN THE DAY FOR SOMEONE ELSE TO LEARN HIS PART. ANYWAY, GOT TO GO. ALMOST AT THE CAR.

Time passed where Andrew had driven her away, and now . . .

Helen: HEY, ARE YOU HOME YET? DON'T YOU START FORGETTING TO TELL ME.

Andrew: YES. SORRY, GOT SIDETRACKED. JUST GOING TO BED. KNACKERED.

Helen: OKAY, SPEAK SOON.

Andrew: BYE!

He stared at Stacey. "Who is Helen?"

She tried to speak, but with a scorched mouth, that was a bit hard.

He giggled. "No matter. I'll find out."

And he left her there, her skin no doubt still burning, each layer roasting.

Good.

* * *

Over the next three days, with Stacey starving and burnt at the secret place, Andrew had many conversations with Helen. He told her the man in the troupe wasn't a creep after all, just a misunderstood bloke, and she was sorry she'd said he was smelly. He couldn't have suspicion falling on him when Stacey never made it home and people started talking. Helen might blab about him as a potential person to worry about.

Each time Helen asked to meet up for a drink, he'd put her off, but the time had come where he couldn't any longer. She'd get suspicious otherwise. Besides, he needed to know who she was.

It was Sunday, and he told her to wait for him at the Shank at eight p.m., seeing as she'd mentioned that pub already a day or so ago.

He waited inside, five minutes early, down by the mouth of the corridor that led to the toilets. A slot machine stood there, so he pressed his side against it. No one would even take any notice of him, although that barmaid — Rita, everyone called her — had got him talking while he'd ordered his Coke, and he'd told her all about his acting. Couldn't stop himself.

To get some idea of who he'd be meeting, he'd discussed outfits with Helen earlier, in that girly way, like Stacey couldn't make up her mind, and wasn't that just the most horrendous dilemma anyone could have, not knowing what jeans or top to put on?

First world problems.

OOOH, WHAT ARE YOU WEARING? I'M NOT SURE WHAT TO PICK.

And there Helen was, in exactly what she'd said, a red, tight-fitting T-shirt and black skinny jeans. High heels.

Long blonde hair.

Andrew jolted at that. He'd planned to just get rid of her as a means to stop her dropping him in the shit, but that hair changed everything.

He'd have to take her skin.

She sat at the bar for a while nursing a clear drink, might be a G and T, might be vodka, then whipped her phone out, and he knew she'd be texting Stacey. Lucky for him, music blared, and Stacey's message tone got swallowed up amidst Lewis Capaldi waffling about letting his guard down.

Helen: WHERE ARE YOU?

Stacey/Andrew: I'M SO SORRY! I WAS SICK. MUST HAVE BEEN SOMETHING I ATE.

Helen: AWW, WANT ME TO COME ROUND?

Stacey/Andrew: NAH, I'M GOING TO BED. NITE.

Helen glanced about, as if checking to see if anyone else she knew was there so she could sit and chat with them. Finding herself lonely as a cloud — bloody hell, LMAO — she left.

Andrew got in the Ford and followed her all the way home.

CHAPTER NINE

Bethany woke from a dream about Victorians, disorientated and groggy, her eyes fighting to stay closed. Her phone rang, shrill in the darkness. She glanced at the glowing numbers on the bedside clock — five a.m. — and grabbed her mobile. Isabelle's name was on the screen.

Shit.

Bethany swiped it. "Morning." Although it still felt like night. She hadn't got to bed until just before one. Four hours was *not* enough.

"Morning to you, too. I'm in the woods where we found Helen Chown. My lot discovered another grave. They've been uncovering the body overnight — I got down here an hour ago once I had confirmation that we definitely *had* a body."

"Is it close to Helen's?"

"A few metres ahead. I'd say they were both buried on the same night or extremely close to that, maybe a night later. The ground hasn't had time to settle with the second body either, like Helen's."

"Female?"

"Yes. Blonde. In a plastic bag. She's got some sort of renaissance dress on instead of Victorian. There's another velvet bag with ID."

"Okay, what's her name and address?"

"Stacey Maxey, thirty-eight Bluebell Drive."

"Right, I'll ring Ursula and get her to do a check. It'll be interesting to see if Stacey has also been reported missing."

"It will. Anyway, up you get. Into the shower. Duty calls."

Bethany managed a laugh, even though she didn't feel in the slightest bit amused. She'd hoped to have slept until seven. Coffee would have to be her best friend today.

After a call to Ursula, she rang Mike to give him the news, then got ready. In her little galley kitchen, she boiled the kettle and slipped a piece of bread into the toaster.

Ursula got back to her. "Yes, a missing person. Reported by her sister and next of kin, Laura MacDonald, after Stacey failed to turn up for their usual Saturday night drink. The notes say Stacey's been gone since Thursday evening, the week before last — so she went AWOL before Helen Chown. She was last seen at the end of a rehearsal for a play she was directing, but her car was gone from the usual spot that she parks in, behind the community centre. The caretaker there was the last to see her, and he was picked up on CCTV walking across the road to his house opposite. Glen Underby did the questioning on that one. Want me to action getting her phone details? Helen's still haven't come through yet."

The fact Helen didn't have a phone in the flat or inside that velvet bag spoke of the abductor taking it. Waiting for phone companies to send call and message information either came quickly or took ages. A lottery of when to expect it.

"Please. I assume Stacey's phone isn't with her. Isabelle didn't say. Right, I need to ring Fran and Leona to ask them to come in a bit earlier. Leona will need to go through the CCTV by the woods again, see if she can spot a car that was in the area on Helen's night, plus another. This is getting a bit too tangled — so much to do and think about."

"I'll leave you to get on then."

Call over, she got hold of Fran and Leona, apologising for the ungodly hour. Bethany made a quick coffee in a to-go cup, one for Mike, too, and scarfed down the buttered toast.

She made it to Mike's inside five minutes, handed his drink over when he jumped in and then got him caught up on all information.

"Leona's better off looking for that car I spotted," Mike said. "The one that was also down Helen's way."

"Message that to her, will you? She can check that one first."

Mike did that, and Leona replied quickly, Mike responding.

"I've let her know the file number and time for that car is on my desk," he said. "It'll save her trawling through it all again." A sip of coffee. "Christ, this is nice. You've changed your brand."

She laughed. He'd know that, having lived with her for a while. "I did. It's fancy instant stuff. Nescafé Azera. Americano."

"Get you. You'll be buying it in Starbucks on the way in next."

"Not likely. Too expensive for my pocket." She paused. "Just thought. I'm not going to bother ringing Tracy Collier this time. She'll know what's going on here, and like she said, if we can manage without her, then we should."

"I think we do pretty bloody well by ourselves. We don't need Serious Crimes poking their noses in."

"Not to mention it'd bruise my ego." She wasn't going to lie about it. Having Collier and her partner, Damon, overcrowding Bethany's patch . . . well, it'd piss her off, to be honest.

"I wouldn't say you have an ego."

"Okay, maybe not an ego. It's more me just wanting us to manage on our own. Tracy did it here, that is, before she moved on, so why should we be any different just because she buggered off to head up Serious Crimes? Anyway, enough of her. I need to get my head straight on this case. Isabelle reckons Helen and Stacey were buried at similar times. Let's say a day or two apart. Both women have weird clothes on — did I tell you that bit?"

"You did. So the killer likes the past? Likes old-fashioned clothing?"

"No idea, but whatever the reason, it really bothers me they've been dressed this way. Probably because we don't know why, and if we knew why, we'd most likely have a whole new avenue to waltz down. As it is, we've got blonde victims, the clothing, the little velvet pouches, the plastic bag they've been buried in, and the cable ties, holly sprig and ribbon on Helen's. I didn't get as far as to ask Isabelle if Stacey's has the same."

"Well, we'll see soon enough."

Bethany turned into the woods, using the same track as before. She waved at Tory Yates standing by the roadside, opened her window so they could sign the log and then drove a short way to park behind the SOCO vans. The crime scene tape was still in place from Helen's discovery, but her tent was now gone, her body removed, and another had been erected in its place farther along.

Togged up, they walked towards it, the sky lightening from dark to grey with the onset of a new day.

"I wonder," Mike said, "if he dug the second grave at the same time as Helen's."

"That would mean he knew he had another body to put in it."

"Not far-fetched, though. Helen was kept somewhere. If we suspect she was taken from her flat Sunday night, that means she'd been burnt in the meantime and then brought here. Wherever he kept her, he could have holed Stacey up there, too. Then there's Claire Ellis. What if the same person has taken her? She's blonde."

"Hmm."

Bethany started to think about late last night. They'd hung around inside Claire's to help the SOCOs, and at one point, she'd complained that they'd found sod all. It looked highly unlikely the killer had even been inside, just nabbed her out the front and dragged her through the park. A chance encounter? Or had he been watching her, waiting for the right moment to strike? Did Claire Ellis know Helen and Stacey?

A laptop had been found at Claire's, which was with digital forensics, seeing as a password was needed to get into the damn thing. Hopefully, there would be something found on there that could help them work out who had abducted Claire.

She'd spotted a photo of who she assumed was Claire with an older man — possibly her father — on the fridge and had taken a picture of it to send on to Ursula, so she could circulate it and ensure all uniforms were on the lookout for the poor woman.

They'd gone back round to Andrew Phillips', Bethany unable to push away the nagging feeling that he'd acted off earlier on. He'd answered, hair sleep-tousled, eyes bleary. Her gut instinct that it might be him must be due to his behaviour and demeanour, plus the fact Claire had reported him. This time, he'd seemed incoherent, perhaps overtired, and her questioning him again about his nighttime activities had brought the same answers.

She'd had to take a step back from her suspicions and allow him to be left in peace.

She sighed. "Yes, all of them being blonde is a concern."

"Do you still have a thing about it being Phillips?" Mike asked.

"Maybe."

Nicola had confirmed with Mr Lutworth that he had spoken to Phillips for quite a while, perhaps an hour. Ursula had got back to Bethany about the five-a-side pitch. She'd found a number to book time slots, and the man who arranged it and locked up the changing rooms after matches said yes, a male had been there, playing with a ball by himself. The pitch bloke had been the last one to leave at about nine, and the male had still been there. So Phillips' timing of arriving home at nine, nine-thirty seemed to be the truth.

But Claire had been taken around ten.

Ursula had also got back to her about the mental health issue. Phillips wasn't down as receiving any form of help, at least not with the charities or NHS personnel who had been inclined to speak to her at that time of night. The fact that they would have broken patient confidentiality wasn't a concern of Bethany's. She wanted answers without the red tape.

Ursula had also discussed things with Kribbs, who'd said he'd sort out the paperwork regarding Phillips' GP, as and when Bethany had a more concrete reason to suspect the man other than him being 'weird'. Ouch. Kribbs didn't usually do the whole barb thing, but Bethany would let him off. He'd been strange for a long while now, and she'd thought he was ill or something. Turned out, he'd had aches and pains from stress — because his wife had fucked off with a woman and set up home in Liverpool.

As for Claire's phone ping being checked, there had been no news as of the early hours when Bethany had crawled into bed.

It reminded her to message Fran and tell her to chase that up, along with liaising with Ursula, then Rob when he took over from her at seven, to push for Helen's and Stacey's call information.

"My head hurts just thinking about all this," Bethany said as they got to the tent.

"I expect Stacey's head hurt as well," Isabelle said from inside. "She's got a bloody great big gash on it, blood drips down her face, and her mouth has been burnt."

Bethany glanced at Mike, his features clear in the glow coming from within the tent: *Oh, fuck me . . .* She nodded: *I feel the same, matey*. Then they stepped inside, Bethany holding her breath for a moment and purposely ignoring the body. She thought about there being no SOCO outside and no torch beams slicing through the undergrowth. They must have done all that yesterday and last night and had thankfully been able to go home. The only remaining officers stood around the body — two of them — while a third knelt, taking pictures.

Isabelle stood beside the others, grinning and appearing as though she'd had a full night's sleep when she hadn't. "Welcome to another madhouse. This poor sod here" — she gestured to the photographer — "really needs to get some kip, so I told him to get on with it and I opened the bag."

Bethany hadn't wanted to see another woman inside a bag. She didn't want to see her out of it either, but that wasn't something she could avoid. For now, though, she would. "Does it have holly, a cable tie and ribbon on it?"

"It does." Isabelle nodded. "So, either another present to us or they've got a thing about prickly leaves." She sighed. "Before I forget — the Claire Ellis scene. The blood from the wall and pavement, plus her shoe, hair, and material sample are at the lab. Reason I mention it is because Aradul was on shift throughout the night, and you know how he likes rushing things through for me."

Aradul was some bloke who'd started six months ago and had a thing for Isabelle. She said jump, he asked how high. In this instance, Bethany was glad of it if he'd put their case before others, but privately, she thought it was cruel if Isabelle was leading him on. She was overly flirty with him, and he must think she was interested.

"And?" Bethany cocked her head.

"I received an email from him about five minutes ago. The wall, pavement and shoe blood match DNA taken from Claire's place — from her toothbrush — and the hair from the hedge. They belong to her. Nothing we weren't expecting, but it's always nice to have something confirmed, isn't it."

Bethany nodded.

The photographer said he'd finished, and Isabelle told them all to go home.

"I've got people coming who've had sleep," she told them. "I don't want to see you lot until tomorrow, bright and early." She paused. "Unless something crops up and we need you in the meantime."

Bethany thought of the three teams Isabelle had on rotation, and how someone was always rested and ready to go. With her own team, being only four of them, they were run ragged a lot of the time, which was why Bethany had sent

Fran and Leona home last night. They needed sharp minds to keep digging the way they did behind the scenes while Bethany and Mike were out in the field.

"Presley will be here in a bit," Isabelle said. "Wasn't happy I woke him up with a chirpy phone call."

"I know the feeling." Bethany smiled. "And I'm now wondering whether we should wait for a decent hour to go and see Stacey's sister."

"Hmm. Your decision. By the way, Stacey's driver's licence was treated the same as Helen's. Blacked-out photo, those odd words. The sister, next of kin, is she?" Isabelle asked. "And are you going to actually look at Stacey anytime soon?"

Bethany let out a ragged breath. "Yes, next of kin, and yes, I'll bloody well look."

She did — and may as well have been staring at Helen Chown. The women were strikingly similar, and it further confirmed to Bethany that whoever had done this to them had a certain type they went after. Claire matched them in features and bone structure, so there was no doubt in Bethany's mind that all three women were linked.

It reminded her they had to go and see Claire's father. Ursula had sent a message with his name and address. Bethany had held off visiting him in the early hours in case Claire was found. With her still missing, there was no choice but to go and see a man who would be devastated at the fact his child had been snatched. Whether she was an adult or young, it didn't matter. Claire was still that man's baby.

A sudden weariness came over Bethany, that the world was so wicked and evil, with so many people in it intent on doing harm to others and destroying more lives than the ones they actually snuffed out. Families, broken, never to be the same again.

It sickened her more than she'd admit. If she let herself be consumed by that disgust, she'd become bitter. Like Vinny had once told her: *Stay you. Don't let them change you.*

While she'd been stuck inside her head, gazing vacantly at Stacey's shell, Presley had arrived. With a grumpy hello, he did his usual sketch of the body and then hunkered down beside it. Isabelle was waffling on at him and probably getting on his nerves, as he likely only had one coffee in his system.

"Blow to the head," he said, cutting her off.

Isabelle had clearly pissed on his cornflakes.

"Marks on her wrists from being bound." He lifted the hem of the dress to inspect Stacey's shoes, which were soft-soled ballerinas in emerald-green. They were the same shade as the majority of the dress, which had a cream panel down the front with laces crisscrossing it on the bodice.

Isabelle said renaissance. Sod living in those times, wearing something like that.

"Ankles, too," Presley went on.

"Different to Helen then," Bethany said. "Unless she had marks on her ankles under her boots?" A slight dig at Presley for not contacting her yet about any findings regarding Helen. Granted, he was probably busy, and maybe he hadn't even started her post-mortem yet, but whatever.

"Perhaps Helen was a different kind of person. Maybe she didn't need tying up to be subdued," Presley said. "She wasn't touched sexually, by the way."

That was something, although the killer had probably been more intent on burning the poor love to be interested in violating her in that way.

"I'm wondering if she was whacked on the head in order for her to be abducted," Bethany said. "Claire Ellis" — she explained to Presley who that was — "bled on the pavement. She'd touched the wound — the blood on the wall was a handprint. She'd shouted in her street before being dragged away. Maybe that shout was from pain."

"I deal with the dead," Presley said. "Claire Ellis isn't a concern of mine until she's no longer living."

"Bloody hell, Elvis," Isabelle said, poking him on the shoulder, "you need to rein it in. We're looking at Claire being the next victim, so she'll be on your radar. You having information about her now can only help later."

Presley harrumphed, probably because she'd called him Elvis, which he hated. "Strangulation marks on the neck. Buried around the same time as Helen Chown."

"I already said that," Isabelle griped.

"Well, I wasn't aware of that," Presley snapped. He lifted Stacey's sleeve. "Burns."

To stop this conversation deteriorating further, Bethany said, "Vague idea of time of death?"

Presley took an ear temp, the air tense while they all waited for the gadget to beep.

"Around the same time as Helen," he said.

The sound of a car filtered in and Isabelle moved to the tent flap. "My people are here."

Bethany took that as their cue to escape. Presley was in too much of a foul mood to hang around. She said goodbye and walked out with Mike.

In the car, she said, "That man is a ball of fun."

"Glad I'm not spending the next hour or so with him — or the rest of the day." Mike slipped his seat belt on. "Christ." He turned to look at her. "Right, Claire's dad first or Stacey's sister?"

"I'm thinking we deal with Claire's situation first. She's potentially still alive, and if we can get some information on where she might be, there's a chance we can save her. Stacey . . . well, she's dead. We can't help her now, and letting her sister remain oblivious in sleep for a while longer sits better with me."

"I agree. Come on then. Let's get this over and done with."

CHAPTER TEN

Andrew stayed in the car, gloves on, and watched Helen cross Potter's Yard. She slid her key in the lock, went inside, and he waited until one a.m., then reversed up to her front door. Left the engine running. Lifted the boot, ready.

He got out and, pulling Stacey's phone from his pocket, tapped out a message.

> *Stacey/Andrew: ARE YOU UP? I'M OUTSIDE. I DON'T FEEL TOO GOOD. CAME OVER SO I WASN'T BY MYSELF.*

He switched the phone off and pushed it into his pocket, then stood there waiting for her to come downstairs — providing she even heard the message tone.

Eventually, the door opened, and Helen appeared. He couldn't see her features, too dark, but imagined shock clambered all over her face.

He wasn't Stacey. She'd registered it.

He shoved her backwards before she had a chance to open that mouth of hers and scream. She staggered, landing on her arse, letting out a whimper. Shutting the door quietly, he advanced on her, taking a rag from his pocket, feeling for her mouth and stuffing it inside.

"I'm taking you to see Stacey. So be quiet, got it?"

She nodded.

"You haven't been talking to her on Messenger all this time." He gripped her arms and lifted her, setting her on her feet. "You've been talking to me. Now, if you want to see your friend, you'll come out to my car and not make a sound. If you disobey, I'll kill her, and you, understand?"

She nodded, snorting, terror settling in for the duration.

"I'm going to take you outside now. Remember . . . silence."

She nodded again, frantic.

He opened the door, pushed her outside, then into the boot. Grabbed the monkey wrench. Gave the back of her head a good fucking whack.

Silence guaranteed.

He shut the boot, locked it and then returned to her flat. Got her handbag, collected her phone from the bedroom and took her laptop. In the kitchen, he looked through the cupboards and found a champagne flute. Smashed the lip. Placed his gift inside.

Perfect.

* * *

Stacey sobbed upon seeing Helen in Andrew's arms. He placed her down on the opposite side of the room to her friend, then got to burning Helen quickly, desperate for her skin. Stacey gargled strange noises throughout, while Andrew gave a running commentary, also telling her if she didn't let their skin touch, if she didn't willingly and lovingly press her naked self to his bare back, she'd be killed.

He forgot to mention she'd be killed anyway.

"You had your chance to be kind to me, and you blew it," he said to Stacey, finished with crisping Helen's arms. "You could have had the honour."

Stacey squinted at him as though not understanding what he'd meant.

He placed the tool down. "It's time to peel you."

She shivered and shook her head, air chuntering out of her nostrils.

Fed up of the mess she was making of her face with her tears and snot, he collected a knife from his crate and stabbed her torso. While she screamed and clutched at the wound, he knelt beside her.

"Now shush. I need peace and quiet to enjoy peeling this."

* * *

Stacey didn't die straight away. In the days spent waiting for Helen's skin to peel, Stacey clung on, having created a compress for the stab wound by bunching up her clothing and pressing it down. She was grey, half in this realm, half in Hell, the place she'd eventually find herself.

Andrew had pasted her skin to the community centre map. He'd drawn a new map, of the woods, a row of trees, and he'd place Helen's skin there once he'd peeled it, at the bottoms of the trunks. It would look like snow on the ground.

He stabbed Helen, remembering doing it to the first woman to suffer a death in this way, the bitch who'd sent him on this path. He must have nicked something important. Helen bled out quickly.

She could have the Victorian dress, the boots and one of the velvet bags that woman *had made. It felt good to find a use for them.*

He cleaned her, dressed her, placed her in a plastic bag. Cable-tied it. Added a bow, the holly — Claire, he'd have her one day, too. She was on his mind all the time, everything about her.

Helen was buried a short distance from the first victim, that woman. *While he was at it, he dug a grave for Stacey. She'd snuff it soon. Didn't do any harm to be prepared.*

CHAPTER ELEVEN

Roger Ellis. He was slim, late fifties, with black hair, a touch of grey smattering it, and a haggard face from where they'd got him out of bed at stupid o'clock. The same man in the photo from Claire's fridge, but this time he stood in an open doorway in shorts and a T-shirt, feet bare.

Bethany produced her ID and introduced them, his cheeks going white, eyebrows rising, then drawing down.

"We're here about your daughter, Claire," she said. "May we come in?"

He frowned. "What's the matter? Has that dickhead finally done something to her? I told you lot before, why wait for actual harm to come to her? Going round there to tell him not to bother her hasn't worked — he's still doing it, you know, only she hasn't reported it again because there's no bloody point. I promise you, if he's done something, and I get my hands on him . . ."

"Inside is best, Mr Ellis." Mike indicated they should go in, glancing up and down the street for effect: *Your neighbours might be listening if they're up.*

Roger stepped back directly into a living room. There were stairs to the left and a door ahead that was open enough to show a silver washing machine beside a sink unit. The draining board was full of washing up stacked in a red plastic stand, something Bethany could do with getting.

Home Bargains at some point then.

Once they were seated, Roger appearing incredibly uncomfortable on the sofa, Bethany let out a slow breath.

"I'm sorry to have to tell you, but we have reason to believe Claire was abducted last night."

Roger shot up, fists clenched, those pale cheeks of his sprouting red blooms. "It's him, isn't it, that fucking weirdo."

"Which weirdo, Mr Ellis?" She'd bet he was going to say Phillips.

"Andrew, that bloke next door. He's always pushing himself on her, wanting her to talk to him, following her places, and all she's doing is trying to read her sodding books, and there he is, at her fence — and sometimes, he climbs over the damn thing. Actually comes up to her *in her own garden* and starts guffing on about all sorts. I'm telling you, if she's been taken, it's him."

Shit.

Bethany would have to go and speak to Phillips again, but with his house already searched by Mike, what else was there to find? Unless they nosed in his garden. And what was there to say that she hadn't already discussed with him? Thinking about it, though, she'd have cause to see him again — he may well have gotten home by nine-thirty, but where had he been between then and when he'd opened the door to them later that night? There was a patch of time that couldn't be accounted for, except for him saying he'd been at home, alone.

"Apart from Andrew," she said, "is there anyone else you can think of who might have wanted to take Claire — and why?"

Roger shook his head. "No one. She doesn't go out much. She's a bookworm, loves nothing more than curling up with a story. There's a group she started on Facebook. She's got a few mates on there, and she sees her brother and sister-in-law often, and maybe Ginny pops round for a cuppa

— that's the neighbour on the other side. Oh, and she's got Katy and Viv. They go to quiz night every week." He paused as though a snippet of info had thumped into his brain. "Hang on, she'd have been at the Shank for that last night."

Mike scribbled that down, then got his phone out, probably to message Fran and Leona.

"Do you know Katy's and Viv's numbers? Where they live?" Bethany asked.

He shook his head. "I don't, but they live close to the Shank, I know that much, because they let Claire walk home by herself. Sorry, but what sort of friends are they? I've said that to Claire, but she won't listen." He paced, running a hand through his hair. "Where did this happen? How do you even know she was taken? Fuck, I can't get my head around this."

"Outside her house," she said. "A neighbour heard a female shouting, so he came out to see what was going on and caught sight of who he thought was Claire being taken down the street and through the hedge bordering the park." She paused, thinking of whether to tell him about the blood. She would. "We think she was struck as there was blood on the pavement — a few spots — and a bloody handprint on the top of her front garden wall. One of her shoes was found in the park, along with hair and material caught on the hedge. We've had the analysis fast-tracked during the night and compared the DNA to that on Claire's toothbrush. It matches."

"Her toothbrush?"

"We were sufficiently alarmed enough to gain entry into her house."

"Oh, bloody hell . . . Do you think . . . Do you think she's alive?"

"We have no reason to believe otherwise at this time," she said. *But I think she might end up dead in the near future if we don't get to her.* "The bloody handprint was Claire's, and we know she was alive when she touched the wall because she was abducted soon after. We have every hope that we can find her and bring her home safely. What we need to do now is learn about her life, who she knew, who she may have offended, however slight, for them to come for her in this way. Or we could be looking at a random grab." *Do I tell him about the other women? Yes, in case he knows of a link.* "She fits the profile of two females we're currently investigating."

"Hang on, two other women?" He brushed a hand over his chin. "Bleedin' Nora, there was that other lady in the news. Helen someone . . ."

Bethany nodded. "I'm afraid they went missing too. Do you know Helen Chown or Stacey Maxey? Do you know if Claire does?"

"No," Roger said.

She glanced at Mike to gauge whether she should say more.

He shook his head.

Unfortunately, Roger caught it. "Hold up a second. What was that about? You shook your head." He pointed at Mike. "What aren't you telling me? Come on, out with it. If something's going on, I want to know the lot. Don't be soft-soaping me."

"We can't discuss it in detail at the moment," she said, thinking of Stacey's sister and how she hadn't been informed of the death yet. "But what I can tell you is that there haven't been favourable outcomes, and we're desperate to find Claire before things take a turn that we'd rather they didn't . . ."

"Shit. *Shit.*" He smacked his forehead with the heel of his hand. "Those other two are dead, aren't they?"

Bethany remained silent.

"My son and his wife are away at the moment. Wales." Roger rubbed his temples. "Should I get them back here? I don't know what to do."

"That's something only you can decide," she said. "If you feel you need family around you, then maybe that's the best option. However, if you'd prefer to keep this quiet in case we find Claire and your son doesn't need the worry . . ." She couldn't make the decision for him. "We do have a Family Liaison Officer who can come and talk things through with you. Her name's Alice Jacobs, and she's an amazing source of comfort and information. She can talk you through all the steps so you know exactly what we'll be doing to find Claire and how long it's likely to take. Would you prefer that?"

He flopped onto the sofa, head in his hands. "Yes, then I haven't got to bother my boy with it just now. They haven't had a holiday in ages — I don't want to ruin that if I don't have to. Like you say, we might get Claire back. I should go out and help with the search."

"No, it's best you remain at home. We will need to know your son's whereabouts so we can discreetly make enquires to check he is where he says he is." She held up a hand when Roger lifted his head to voice a complaint. "We don't for one minute think it's him, but we have to check. Do you understand?"

"Yeah."

"Do you know exactly where your son is?"

"The Quay Hotel & Spa, Conwy. I know that because he recommended it to me, and I went there last year."

"Thank you. What's his name? And that of his wife?"

He offered that information, then, "So what about the dickhead? What's being done about him?"

"If you're talking about Andrew Phillips, we have spoken to him twice and also to people who saw him around that time. We've searched his home — it was voluntary, he allowed us inside without complaint." To stop Roger from going there and punching the man's lights out or asking him questions, she said, "Nothing untoward was in his house; even the loft was checked. We're satisfied, for the moment, he was where he said he was." *For the moment*: she'd said that so there was no comeback from Roger later down the line if it *did* turn out to be Phillips.

"I'll ring Alice and the others," Mike said and left the room.

"Who are the others?" Roger asked.

"Our colleagues. He'll be passing on the information about your son and daughter-in-law, Katy and Viv, Claire possibly being at the Shank, and Ginny, the neighbour, will be spoken to again."

"Blimey, you don't hang about, do you?"

"No. We can't afford to." She smiled sadly. "Just know there are many of us working on this, and we're all doing everything we can to find Claire. Alice will explain to you about the time that passes, though. You may get frustrated, thinking we're taking too long, but I assure you, if we have to work around the clock, we will."

"I appreciate that."

"Now, in order for our investigation to run smoothly, I'm asking you *not* to go and see Andrew Phillips. Despite the complaints Claire made about him, while we have no proof he's involved, we have to just monitor the situation." *And my boss isn't allowing me to get heavy with Phillips until I have something else to go on, fuck it.* "While we may have suspicions about people, we can't be seen to harass them." *Much as I'd like to.*

"So from what you've just said, monitoring the situation . . ." He nodded. "I'm only going to stay away from him because it might impact Claire. I've kept out of it so far regarding him because she asked me not to cause a fuss, but she did say once that I wasn't to approach him again because he's weird or odd, something like that. To me, that says she was either worried the arsehole would do something to me, or to her. That's been worrying me ever since she said it. But she's an adult, and I can't keep treating her like my little girl. Now I wish I'd ignored her and given the prat a warning."

Mike came back, bearing a cup of tea for Roger.

"Cheers." Roger took the drink. "What's going on now then?"

Mike looked at Bethany, and she dipped her head once to let him know he could explain.

"The other members of our team will be contacting the owner of the Shank, plus Viv and Katy." Mike sat. "I've just had word that digital forensics have been looking at Claire's laptop and gathering information. We don't have the report just yet, so I can't tell you anything. However, our colleagues are on it, and we'll pass any information to Alice so she can tell you what's going on. She'll be here in about two minutes. She lives a few streets away."

Roger sipped some tea. "I'm trying not to think about where Claire is. What's being done to her. It's . . . I don't want to entertain it, but it keeps coming into my head. What if he hurts her? I can't stand to think of her in any pain." His face scrunched up.

The doorbell dinged, and Mike got up to answer it. Alice came in, and after introductions, Bethany and Mike left Roger with her. Having Alice there would also give assurance that Roger didn't leave the house to rip Phillips a new one.

In the car, she sighed and pulled away from the kerb. "Phillips?"

"I know," Mike said, "but we can't hound the bloke. We have nothing on him."

"I want to put someone outside his house to watch him, but Kribbs isn't going to agree to that. Can't afford to have someone under guard, Phillips hasn't done anything as far as we know, blah fucking blah. Meanwhile, if it's him, he could be doing all manner of things to Claire and also lining up his next victim."

"Hmm. It's frustrating. What I didn't say back there . . . I lied about not getting any reports. Digi have found a conversation Claire had with members of her Facebook group. She's told them all about him. I've had the screenshots sent to me. Pull over so we can read them."

Bethany drove on until a lay-by appeared. She parked, and Mike took his phone out and brought the info up. Bethany leant over so she could read it.

> Claire Ellis: Hi, my lovelies. I've got a bit of a problem, and I need some advice. My next-door neighbour is a right weirdo, and I'm sick to death of him. He's stolen my knickers — a few pairs now — and keeps coming into my back garden . . . in his dirty pants! I've told the police about him because he also keeps turning up in places where I go, and I'm

starting to feel like I want to punch him one. The police won't do anything.

> Kay Bee: OMG, what a weirdo! [SHOCKED EMOJI]

Romy Brown: What? The police won't do anything?

> Karen Davies: Um, that's a bit worrying. What do you mean by dirty pants? Please don't say it's what I think it is. My breakfast might not stay down. [QUEASY FACE EMOJI]

Michelle Atkinson: Stolen your knickers? That's seriously odd. How do you know it's him, though? Did you see him doing it?

> Lorraine KJ: Aww, I'm so sorry you're going through this. [LOVE HEART] [KISSY FACE]

Claire Ellis: Romy Brown No, they won't do anything unless he causes me harm or threatens me. That doesn't give me much hope. Seems I just have to put up with him.

Claire Ellis: Karen Davies His pants . . . They have shit on them. [POO EMOJI]

Claire Ellis: Michelle Atkinson I just know it's him. Who else would take them off my washing line? And he's always in my garden. He climbs over the bloody fence! OMFG, I don't believe it! He's here right now.

Claire Ellis: [PHOTO OF A MAN IN UNDERPANTS LEANING ON HER FENCE INSIDE HER GARDEN]

Claire Ellis: See? He's just climbed over and is standing there. I've asked him to leave, but he's ignoring me. I'm sitting here reading.

Romy Brown: Claire Ellis But that's too late to wait for him to hurt you. Bloody hell! [ANGRY EMOJI]

Karen Davies: Claire Ellis Poo? OMG.

Emma Smart: Get hold of the police now and send them that photo. You've got proof he's on your property!

Rosey Goodwin: Wow. That would frighten me. I'm worried about you. There must be something we can do.

Claire Ellis: Rosey Goodwin Apparently wait until he does something to me, that's what I can do. I've been offered a restraining order, but for God's sake, he lives next door. We're going to bump into each other when we leave our houses.

Lorraine KJ: Then the police need to issue one that says he can't come into your garden. And I don't want to scare you, but it sounds like he's following you if he's in the same places you are.

Michelle Atkinson: Lorraine KJ I thought the same thing. Stalker or what!

Sharon Craig: I'm heaving at poo on his pants. Why? And why is he even walking round in just pants? I don't get it.

Angela Cockburn: That is just disgusting — him and the police not doing anything about it. You should be safe in your own home, not worried. Hug xx

Yvonne Seabourne: Whaaaat? This is like something you watch on TV. Do you have a house alarm? Can you get a camera set up?

Claire Ellis: Thanks, everyone. It's nice to finally talk to someone other than my dad about it. Yvonne Seabourne I'm going to get a higher fence so he can't climb over. At the moment, it's only waist height. And I've been thinking about a camera.

Leslie Mills: Just been reading all this. Claire Ellis Definitely get a camera, but in the meantime, what about recording him on your phone? You need to build up a diary of what he's up to. If this is happening on a daily basis, if you have times and dates written down, and video footage, pictures, surely the police will have to take it seriously.

Claire Ellis: Leslie Mills Yeah, I'll do that. Great idea. Thanks!

Bethany looked at Mike. "I feel bloody awful. I can see their point. It looks like we haven't done anything for her, but we have rules, restrictions, and as much we'd like to sort things for people, we can't. In light of what's happened . . ."

"Don't you dare go blaming yourself. Claire did the right thing in reporting him. I'm coming round to the idea it's him — actually, fuck it, it *is* him — but again, we're restricted. Unless we bring him in for questioning to find out where he was between nine-thirty and after Claire was abducted . . . But he's already stated he was at home, and the bloke who saw someone dragging her away didn't see who it was."

"We're stuck, but I do want to speak to him again anyway. I'll force the issue on the missing time and watch for his reactions, but we need to get to Laura MacDonald's and break the news about her sister first." She sighed. "What an almighty fucking mess."

CHAPTER TWELVE

Claire had spent the night flicking between dozing and staring out through the glass in the door. Daylight was on the way, the sky going from black to grey to a muddy peach. Birds twittered, heralding the start of a new kind of torture — waiting for him to come back and not knowing what he was going to do to her. She hadn't fired up her Kindle again, but now, fraught with nerves, she needed something to take her mind off this situation. *If* she could even concentrate on the words, that was.

SCENARIO SEVENTEEN

Necessity: A Holiday. Be on friendly terms.

NEEDED:
HOLIDAY LOCATION
LENGTH OF ROPE
A CLIFF
A CARAVAN AWAY FROM OTHERS

Hey, it's time to go farther afield. What better place than a destination where you're both on unknown soil, away from the strains of your street and all the angst it brings? You're still fake-pally with your neighbour and suggest you take a holiday together. Of course, your neighbour must be as single as you — no spouses or children to worry about. Off you go, driving to a campsite where they have static caravans. You wanted one at the edge of the park, you told the booking woman. You'd like to enjoy your break as far away from humanity as you can. To recharge. The booking lady had sighed, said that sounded like Heaven on Earth, and she had just the right van for you.

There you are, unloading your suitcases from the boot of your car — it's fine to take yours this time. After settling in the caravan, each admiring the bedrooms — let the neighbour have the double so there's more space for what comes later — you make a nice meal on the tiny cooker. Dinner out of the way, you suggest an evening at the clubhouse. People will see you together, and you must make a show of getting along. Oh, how you'll laugh and smile, and everyone will know you're best buddies. Planting the seeds for later is essential, as on this occasion, you'll be questioned by the police. That'll add a bit of spice to things, won't it?

The band playing at the clubhouse is a roaring success, and you manage to drag your neighbour onto the dance floor, again getting seen. No one can dispute the way you interact — it's clear you bear no animosity towards the person who has been pissing you off at home.

At the end of the night, you walk along with a few others, chatting away, then everyone peels off to their own caravans. Your neighbour goes to bed, while you ensure you have gloves on and your rope handy. Let an hour pass. Go into your neighbour's room. Let's not imagine they wake up and make a nuisance of themselves. Here, in this kill fantasy, you're able to slip the rope around their neck and pull both ends tight, strangling the little bastard until they're dead.

There's a cliff behind your caravan, and you wait another hour, the corpse's face contorted, tongue hanging out.

Then you manage to haul them to the edge of the cliff. The sea churns, smacking into the rocks, white spume frothy. With the rope tossed over into the depths, your neighbour follows via a healthy kick in the backside. You watch them sail down and disappear into the waves, then rush back to your caravan, stash the gloves in your case, and get into bed to give the impression you've been asleep. We need ruffled covers and sheets here, a dip in the pillow.

Ten minutes pass.

Then, oh, is that a noise you hear? Someone breaking in? You call the front desk — they're open twenty-four seven for their guests, God bless them — and tell them there's an intruder. You promise the woman you'll stay in bed, too scared to move, but in reality, you're up, opening the caravan door using a tea towel to cover your hand so it looks like it was left that way in a hurry by someone else.

Put the tea towel away, then get back between the sheets.

The campsite security arrive, as do the police, and they find you in a ball on your bed, scared out of your wits.

"My friend!" you say. "Are they all right?"

Their search for them is underway while you're questioned. No, you don't know where they could have gone. Yes, there was the sound of someone opening the main door. No, you didn't think it was your friend because they'd been asleep for a while.

On and on it goes.

Later, the neighbour washes up on the rocks.

To cut a long story short, you get away with it.

Gold star. Well done!

If Claire killed Andrew, would she get away with it? Could she claim self-defence? How would she even get him to take the bonds off her wrists and ankles so she could use the rope to throttle him like in the book?

Skin. She'd have to promise he could touch hers. She'd have to do what that killer did in Scenario Seventeen and pretend to like him. Make him think he had a chance with her. Something, anything to gain his trust and get him to release her.

She'd have to perform the biggest act of her life.

A sound. Something like a key sliding in a lock. Then he was there, standing in the room, staring across at her. He held a wooden crate and placed it down in the opposite corner. Took an item out and set it on top. Some kind of tool in a stand.

"Do I need to use this, Claire Bear?" he asked, pointing at it.

"Wh-what is it?" Her voice, so croaky. Shit, she needed a drink. "Water?"

"That's being rude," he said. "Don't ask for anything. *I* decide when you can have a drink or food. And that decision all depends on whether you're good or not."

"I'll be good," she said, hating herself for what she'd said. For how she'd said it. Pleading. Desperate. "I'll do whatever you want." She remembered Scenario Seventeen. "Why didn't you just say you wanted to touch my skin? I mean, before, at home? I would've let you."

"No, you wouldn't. You kept telling me to go away. 'Get out of my garden!' That's what you said. And, 'Are you fucking following me?' And, 'I'll bloody ring the police on you!' Those aren't kind words. Those don't give me hope that I can have your skin." He stared at her. "And this will make *sure* I have your skin. You'll burn."

Her heart rate went mental, and she struggled to breathe evenly. Now she looked at the tool properly, it was some kind of heat gun. Shit. God, no. No, he wouldn't use that . . .

"Your skin will peel," he said. "And it'll go on the map."

The map?

"No, you don't need to burn me," she said. "Please, just touch me. It's okay."

He fished something else out of the crate. Oh my God, it was her Christmas knickers. She went cold, a pit opening up in her stomach. He put them on over his jeans and moved closer. Got down on his knees. Leant in. Pressed his cheek to hers. And, fuck, she wanted to scream. His skin, so clammy, his smell . . . She held back a heave and closed her eyes. Shuddered from disgust.

"Do you like that, Claire? Do you like my *skin*?"

He hissed that last word, his hot breath fanning her ear. A shout of *Get the hell away from me!* pushed to come out, and she struggled to contain it. He moved his head, and his skin slid over hers — he was sweating, or oily, she didn't know which. Her stomach contracted, and she gagged.

He snatched himself away, rising to stand, staring down at her. The green ribbon on the knickers wobbled. "You don't like it."

"I do, I just . . . I can't exactly touch you back." She lifted her bound wrists.

"You think I'm stupid."

"No, I—"

"Yes, you do. You think I'll untie you, then you can get away."

"That's not it at all. Please, please, I—"

"No, Claire. It's time for the burn."

CHAPTER THIRTEEN

Bethany parked up outside Laura's and took a moment to check her messages.

"Here we go then," she said. "Leona's spotted a car near the woods on the night after Helen had been buried. Same shape and shade as the other one that could possibly have been there previously and also at Potter's Yard on the Sunday."

"Yep, I had a feeling they were one and the same," Mike said.

"It's a bugger we can't get a clear look at the number plates, though. She says it appears to be a Ford. She made out the shape of the logo thingy on the back."

"Well, that's something we didn't know before."

"She's running a check on Ford cars as we speak. Also, Fran spied a link between Helen and Stacey on Facebook, although Stacey hadn't called herself that on there, which was why Fran hadn't picked up on their friendship earlier when digging into Helen's social media. Stacey is down as S M, but in a conversation with Helen on her page a couple of months back, Helen had referred to her as 'Stace'."

"The fact these two know each other is something to go on," he said. "At last."

"*And* the fact that S M also worked at Tips and Talons. Fran said they'd talked about some new gel polish that was coming in and they couldn't wait to try it on the customers. I'm naffed off we didn't get around to questioning that lot sooner. The nail women. We'll make that our next port of call once Stacey's sister has been informed. So, it's likely that if Helen and Stacey knew each other, they possibly knew their killer. Now, does Claire know them? It's not looking that way at the moment, but who knows what might come up in the future. If we'd have gone to the nail salon before now, we'd have known Stacey worked there because, quite frankly, someone would have mentioned it was odd that two employees hadn't turned up for work. We missed a trick there."

"Yes, but we had so much going on and hadn't planned to question the boss and employees until today anyway. Now it's just bumped it up the list — plus going to see the woman who was meant to have her nails done at home by Helen on the Monday."

"Okay, delegate that to a uniform — seeing the family friend."

Mike rang Rob on the front desk and sorted that. "Nicola's going round there."

"Fab. Let's go in and see what this Laura has to say. Maybe she'll know how well Helen and Stacey knew each other. Funny, because Fay Chown never said her daughter had a friend called Stacey."

"Ah, but she did mention the work colleagues."

"Fair enough."

On the pavement, Bethany peered around. Nice street, tidy gardens, clean windows. Some people were leaving for work, suited up, others in casual clothes. A woman struggled to get her children in the car, harassed for the school run. She was red-faced and her expression a picture of: *Why did I have kids again?*

Number two Kiln Gardens was a three-bed by the look of it, yellow and cream daffodils dancing in a circle on the patch of grass masquerading as a front garden — all they needed was handbags in the middle and they'd be eighties ladies on a night out. A path led to the door, a line of grey patio slabs with black shingle between, and Bethany knocked.

A blonde woman answered, lightweight blue jacket on, a bag strap on her shoulder, clearly about to set off for the day. She stopped short and gave a tentative smile that held a question: *Yes?*

Bethany showed her identification. "DI Bethany Smith, and this is my partner, DS Mike Wilkins. We're here regarding your sister, Stacey Maxey."

"Oh, have you found her?" Hope lit up her blue eyes. "Did she just go off for some 'me' time in the end? She said she'd do that once. You know, just have a week or so to herself, no internet or whatever."

"Can we come in?"

"Erm, yes . . ."

She took them to a kitchen done out in high-gloss black, the lingering smell of toast and coffee reminding Bethany it had been ages since they'd had a brew. Thankfully, Laura had obviously been brought up to stick the kettle on as soon as a guest arrived and, seeming in no hurry to get to work or to tell them she had to go elsewhere, she took three white cups off the mug tree and sorted teabags.

"I'm doing this because I know something's wrong," Laura said. "Making drinks, I mean. And if I don't do it, I'm going to cry. I said Stacey mentioned taking off, but honestly, she wouldn't actually do it without letting at least me know. Our parents went out without saying where they were going and ended up dead in a car accident, so Stacey knows she needs to tell me where she's at if she's doing anything out of the ordinary. That's why I reported her missing."

"You carry on doing that while we talk," Bethany said. "Whatever you're comfortable with." She sat at the table so she could watch how the woman behaved — not that she believed Laura had anything to do with this. And sodding hell at her parents being dead. This was going to be tough for her.

Mike sat beside Bethany and took his notebook and pen out.

"Tell us a bit about Stacey," Bethany said.

Laura spooned sugar into the cups. "She's a nail technician, works in Tips and Talons. She's also an actress — or actor as she keeps reminding me they're called these days — and directs plays. One is due to start showing at The Shadwell Theatre next week, so naturally, those who are involved are wondering where Stacey is because the last anyone saw her was the Thursday after a dress rehearsal. That was Jeffrey Velps, the caretaker — I went to see him, seeing as the police weren't doing anything." She turned and smiled sheepishly. "Sorry, that wasn't a dig at you."

"No offence taken. We understand the public's frustration. We're just as frustrated by the red tape. It seems like we're not bothered, but we are. Rules, you see."

"I get it, but when it's your sister, and she's all you've got left . . . Well, you get a bit worried."

"Definitely. What time did Mr Velps see Stacey?"

Laura poured boiled water into the cups and did the business of squeezing the teabags. "About tenish. He said he spoke to her about some of Stacey's skin."

What the fuck? "Um, come again?"

Laura brought their cups over and placed them on the table. "Stacey has a habit of picking sunburn. She'd been to Tenerife." She collected her own cup, putting it on the table. Dropping her bag to the floor and removing her jacket to hang it over the back of her chair, she sat. "Jeffrey saw her talking to one of the actors after a rehearsal. He said he'd looked through the glass in the door because he wanted to lock up and get home, but they were taking their time. Stacey was picking her sunburn. After she'd gone, Jeffrey said he went back to the rehearsal room to see if the man had left, and he found him scooping Stacey's skin up onto a bit of paper, folding it, then putting it in his pocket. Now that is just odd."

Bethany's neck hairs stood up. Odd wasn't the right word. Fucking freaky described it better. Why would anyone want skin? Which brought to mind the burns on the victims. Did they have a skin collector here or what?

She took a sip of tea, then asked, "What happened after he spoke to Stacey about the skin incident?"

"Well, she had a right go at the bloke who'd taken it." Laura laughed. "I can see her doing it an' all. She told him he'd be off the troupe if he didn't buck his ideas up, something like that."

So he could have got the hump and killed her.

But that doesn't explain Helen or Claire.

"Do you have a name for this man?" Bethany sucked in a breath.

"He calls himself George Bernard Shaw, can you believe."

So he wishes he was someone of note?

That was thought-provoking. This person could see themselves as insignificant from treatment during their life or just a general feeling of not being worthy, and they'd reinvented themselves, became an actor to be someone else from time to time. However, unless they'd changed their name by Deed Poll, George Bernard Shaw gave them exactly sod all, and even if they *had* changed it legally, Deed Poll didn't have to give out the information of the previous name.

"Has the troupe continued meeting and rehearsing since Stacey's been missing?" Bethany asked.

Laura shook her head. "According to Jeffrey, no. Stacey rings to book the hall, and she hadn't, so obviously there was no rehearsal. Everyone turned up last week to do their thing, and Jeffrey had to tell them Yoga with Dogs had taken up the time slot."

Yoga with your dog . . .

Mike smothered a smile behind his hand, then turned professional again. "Do you know if the man, George, left at the same time as Stacey?"

Laura shook her head again. "I don't, sorry."

"Which community centre is it?" Mike said.

"The one on this estate."

"Do you know of anyone who would want to harm your sister?" he enquired, tapping the end of the pen against his cheek.

"What are you saying?" Laura looked from him to Bethany.

It was time. *Bollocks.* "I hate to bring bad news, but we found a body in the early hours. We have reason to believe, based on the ID, that it's Stacey."

Laura's tea went flying, the liquid spreading across the table. Mike sprang up to get paper towels, and while Laura stood and clutched at her hair, wailing, Bethany gathered the woman in her arms and held her tight, shuddering with the effect of Laura's sobs. It seemed to go on forever, the crying, and Mike had mopped up the spill long before Laura composed herself.

"There's no one left," she said. "It was just me and Stace."

"Do you have a partner we can call?" Bethany asked, easing Laura back into her seat.

"I'm divorced."

"A friend?" Bethany prodded. Nasty as it sounded, they had to get out of here and visit this Jeffrey Velps bloke to find out what had gone on that Thursday night. The priority was finding Claire — and the killer.

"Christine next door. Christine Robinson." Laura sniffed.

"Which side?" Mike asked.

"Number three. She lives with our friend, Susan Pola, so if Christine isn't in . . ."

"I'll go and get either of them now," he said and walked out.

"Where is she?" Laura asked. "Stacey."

"In the woods, love. She'd been buried." Bethany felt sick. Telling people things like this was bloody horrific.

"How . . . ?"

"We don't know how she died yet." Bethany took a card out of her pocket and placed it on the table. "This lady is called Alice Jacobs. She's with someone else right now, but if you need her, give her a ring. She'll make an appointment to call round."

Laura nodded absently.

Bethany pressed on. "I need to ask whether you're aware that a lady called Helen Chown also went missing."

"Stacey's work friend?" Laura frowned.

"Yes, her disappearance has been on the news."

"I don't watch it."

"She went missing after Stacey, but Helen's body was found before your sister's. They were buried metres apart. We believe the same person took them. Do you know of anyone they'd both know who would do this?"

Laura shook her head. "No. Helen wasn't involved with the troupe, so it can't be George who took her. Stacey met her through work."

"Do you know anyone at all, apart from perhaps George, who would have a grudge against Stacey?"

"No one."

"Sorry to bombard you with questions, but have you ever heard the name Claire Ellis?"

"No."

Mike came back with a black-haired woman who favoured dark clothing and pretty makeup.

"What's happened, Laura?" she asked, rushing over, pulling a chair across and sitting beside her.

"Oh, Christine . . ."

While Laura rambled to her friend, Bethany made a fresh cup of tea for them, but not for herself and Mike. They needed to be away from here. She took the drinks over, ensured Laura was aware she could contact them for help at any time, and then they left. Bethany was feeling hollowed out, her own grief giving her a pinch in the gut to remind her it was still there. Less defined these days, but there all the same.

She drove away, heading for the community centre. "What did you make of that little lot then?"

Mike took his phone out. "That we're a bit closer to finding out who this is. I'm going to message Fran, give her that name. George Bernard Shaw, for God's sake." He tapped his screen.

"I'm eager to hear what this Jeffrey has to say. I want to know who left first that night — George or Stacey."

"Hmm. If this George is in the frame, that puts Phillips right out of it."

"Maybe Phillips is just a weirdo after all."

"Or maybe George took Helen and Stacey, Phillips took Claire, and because it's happened around the same time, we're thinking it's one person."

"I've got no bloody idea at the moment. Once we've seen Jeffrey, we'll nip somewhere for a coffee and talk this through, providing Fran, Leona, or Isabelle don't get hold of us. Plus, I could do with a caffeine injection. I'm already flagging. Then we need to go to Tips and Talons."

She parked outside the community centre, and they entered through a glass door with metal squares embedded in the pane. A playschool was in full swing inside the main room, little ones haring about or playing nicely at various stations: a kitchen, a puzzle table, a water trough standing on a plastic sheet, the kids there wearing various coloured aprons that covered their arms and fronts.

A woman approached from inside and unlocked the door. She stuck her head in the gap. "Can I help you?"

"We're looking for Jeffrey Velps. Is he about?" Bethany smiled.

"Ah, he'll be at home, but he only lives opposite. Number ten."

"Thanks."

They made their way there, and Jeffrey offered for them to go in, but Bethany declined. She asked him questions about the night of the skin being taken, then Stacey going missing, and he related the story Laura MacDonald had told them.

"Who left first out of the two?" Bethany asked.

"George, about ten minutes before Stacey. She hung around in case George waited outside for a lift. She usually took him home but had taken to not doing that. Said he smells and she wasn't comfortable with him lately."

Interesting. "Did she stop wanting to give him a lift before or after the skin incident? What I mean by that is him removing her skin from the premises."

"The night he took that, they got along fine. Talked for ages, which pissed me off, if I'm honest, because it went over her paid time slot, and I wanted to get home. That night, she didn't give him a lift either. I was watching, see. She went down the alley like she always does — she parks out the back there on the street. He walked off down that way." Jeffrey pointed to his right, which would be left out of the community centre.

"Okay, any CCTV around here?"

"Nope. Kids keep vandalising it, so we gave up." He shrugged.

Wonderful. "Thank you for your time."

They crossed the road.

"Let's go along this alley," Bethany said. "I want to get a feel for where she went to get into her car."

They walked down it, refuse bins to the right-hand side. At the end was a street with a field stretching on for what seemed forever.

"Remote," Mike said. "Easy to abduct someone here."

"I thought the same."

They returned to the car, and Bethany zoomed off towards Bottoms Up Bistro. They may as well get *that* off their list an' all while they grabbed a coffee. Someone working that evening would have seen Claire eating there. And Andrew.

"Once we've spoken to the folks at the bistro, we'll go to Tips and Talons, then the Shank," she said.

Bethany hoped Rita had been working behind the bar the night Claire had attended the quiz. Rita had been helpful in a previous case — someone who listened and picked up all manner of things.

Here's hoping she comes up trumps this time, too.

CHAPTER FOURTEEN

Claire's arms hurt. Burned. Even though he'd held the heat quite far away, her skin was turning red. Tears streaked her face, and she had no voice left. She'd screamed it all away.

He stood there, right in front of her, the tool back in its stand on the crate, and played with the green ribbon on her stolen knickers. He was like some macabre Superman with them on over his jeans.

"Does it feel good, Claire Bear?" Head tilt.

I hate you. I'm going to kill you.

She opened her mouth to answer him and tried saying the words: *Fuck off, you absolute maniac!* but only a breath came out, a pitiful puff that said: *You've almost made me want to give up. To die. You've almost broken me.*

Almost. A nugget of strength remained, small, and all but wiped out with the pain, but if she used her hatred to help it grow, she'd get the energy to strive for survival.

For now, she'd rest. Block out the intensity in her arms.

"I have six pairs of your knickers." He rubbed his crotch.

I know.

"Some are cotton, some are silk, and some are lace."

You're sick.

"They feel good. I wear them sometimes. Not like this." He flicked a finger at his jeans. "But against me. On my *skin.*"

She couldn't hold back a shudder.

"That excites you?"

It revolts me.

"Then we're getting somewhere."

I'm going nowhere. Except home.

"Why aren't you talking to me, Claire?" She tilted her head the other way.

She mouthed: *Can't.*

Thought: *Because I don't want to.*

"Oh. I see. You can't speak. Like the others. That's what happens when you scream too much. I'm not sorry you screamed. It makes the burn even better when I hear them."

He's done this before. To someone else.

How many?

Where are they now?

"Is it hurting?" He stroked the Christmas knickers, circling a fingertip around a holly sprig.

She nodded.

"Badly?"

She shook her head.

"Then we should burn you some more. It has to hurt, your soul has to hurt, don't you understand that?"

No! Wait. I mean, yes, it hurts badly. Please don't do this.

He walked to the crate and picked up the tool. Switched it on. The blue flame burst out, the force of it creating a straight line with a turquoise tip. "There. We're ready to go again."

The heat on top of the already raw skin — my God, unbearable. He held the tool steady, not one tremble of his hand, proving he wasn't fazed by what he was doing to her. He didn't care how much agony she was in and appeared to be enjoying it.

She silently shrieked, lips stretching to the point of cracking from lack of a drink for so long, although it was nothing compared to her arm. Her gums ached, her eyes strained, and she stared at where he pointed the flame. Her skin stank, like roast pork, and the hairs on her arms fizzled into nothing.

She was blistering at the spot where the heat was concentrated.

"Watch how it rises in a pretty bubble," he said. "Fascinating."

She couldn't look away. Transfixed, the pain upping to such a degree she somehow didn't feel it anymore, just a throbbing, bloating, stretching sensation, Claire waited for the bubble. Her skin turned yellow in that patch, then rose, filling with . . . something, creating the bubble he'd wanted. He moved the flame, and more skin lifted, the smell getting worse, him repeating the process until a huge dome the size of a tennis ball sat on her arm.

For a moment she had no thoughts. Nothing. Her mind and body frozen. Then . . .

"And now for the right," he said, moving to stand there.

Her brain kicked back into gear. Fresh pain this time, building and building until, once more, she couldn't feel it. Not there, but it returned to the first side, staggering warmth, biting, burrowing down through the fat layer to the muscles, the sinews, the bone.

"It hurts badly now, doesn't it?" he asked.

She nodded along with those silent screams and, mercifully, he switched the tool off. Returned it to its base, placing them on the floor.

She had matching bubbles now. Ugly things. Proof of his madness. Proof of her inability to defend herself.

She sobbed at her weakness.

"That's going to peel lovely." He ferreted about in the crate, taking something out.

She couldn't see for tears. Couldn't close her mouth to stop that non-existent wail coming out of her. Vision fuzzy, she sensed him step closer, and blinked, needing to see what he was going to do next. He stood, one leg either side of hers, and leant over.

"Pop!" He jabbed something into a bubble.

Liquid oozed, hot, like spilt, scalding tea, down her arm towards her hand. A new kind of discomfort, sharp and wicked, streaked into her upper limbs. He burst the second bubble, and she couldn't take any more. Neck cords straining, the bones there hurting with the force of her soundless yowls, she stared at him, hoping hate showed in her eyes, contempt, disgust, but most of all payback. She prayed, when she finally killed this bastard, that he suffered and wished for death quicker than it came. That the reaper took his time in claiming him.

Retribution was sometimes hell, though, and she'd have to go through it before she could fix this. Make it right. Get justice. His treatment of her this morning, his slow torture in the past — the stealing, the violation of her personal space, the stalking — building up to this moment where right now . . . Hell. That was life on Earth. Secretly lethal. Evil. But she'd get through it. She would.

She had to.

Blackness crowded in, slithering from the edges, covering her, until all that was left was his face, hanging there, a mad gleam in his eyes, a smile stretching his thin, sinister lips.

He licked them.

* * *

Claire came to, immediately checking if he was there.

She was alone — as far as she could tell anyway — and for a moment, she felt nothing, then . . . everything. Her arms; it was as though something ate them, chomping at her flesh. She should hurt more than she did, though. Had he given her something to alleviate the pain? Put a salve on her wounds?

With no clue as to how many seconds, minutes, or hours had passed, she relied on the sky to tell her. The grounds out the back weren't facing the sun, so she couldn't see it to gauge the time by its height. When it came round later, she'd know.

Perhaps it was nine o'clock. Ten. Eleven. Maybe a whole day and night had passed, her out of it, her body refusing to let her wake while it tried its best to heal.

Did it even matter?

Yes, it fucking matters. I'm getting out of here.

Her stomach griped. She'd never been this hungry before, so the sensation was new and alarming. Unseen hands wrung out her guts, squeezing, twisting, prodding, then relaxing. Hollow now, a great space inside her, gaping, needing food to fill it, a yawning, infinite void.

She gave talking a go, calling out to him, but again, no sound other than her ragged breaths. Steeling herself, she inspected one arm. Still hot, still burning. The deflated blister was drying, same as the other.

Mouth dry, she swallowed, and God, that hurt.

She reached to her side, gritting her teeth to get through the distress moving brought, and picked up her Kindle. Switched it on.

Forty-seven percent battery.

Would she escape before it ran out?

SCENARIO EIGHTEEN

Necessity: Close enough to strike.

NEEDED:
THUMBS
A KNEE
HANDS
YOUR WITS
MASK
GLOVES

You're in a situation where you're ready to confront your neighbour about their annoying habits. You know, the ones that have you thinking of murder, dreaming of it, waiting for the day you can commit it. You need to be somewhere without witnesses — obvs! — and where shouting, possible screams, and the grunts of a fight won't be picked up.

Let's set this scene. Of course, yours might be different, but this one right here works for me.

You've been doing a spring clean, getting rid of a few things, dumping clutter in favour of the minimalistic approach. You suggest your neighbour does the same, and they agree, wholeheartedly throwing themselves into the task — with a bit too much gusto, if we're honest, but whatever. You've borrowed a van to take all your unwanted belongings to the tip, so you offer to take theirs, too, although they must come with you.

"I'm not some muscle wo/man who can lug everything by myself," you joke, tacking a laugh on the end for kicks.

They don't find it funny, but fuck 'em. You know a good quip when you hear one. That's always been the problem, hasn't it? Their lack of a sense of humour. Why wouldn't they find it funny when you have your Metallica up loud? Why wouldn't it be amusing when you mow your grass at six a.m. on a Sunday morning?

God, some people . . .

Off you both go, and you know, once you get to your destination, you're going to be turned away. After all, the tips these days, most of them require car registration numbers so you can leave your rubbish there on record instead of getting away with disposing of a body chopped up inside several black bags. Blimey, those councils. Paranoid or what!

The van isn't registered with them, so, as planned, you have to go elsewhere.

"Oh no! What a pest! Where shall we get rid of it all now?" you ask, pretending to think, pulling on some gloves. "Ah, I know . . ."

You drive to the woods, travelling deep to where the trees are thick, just like Scenario Fifteen (reminder: spiffing knife jab to the throat). The pair of you get out, and as your neighbour's things were the last to be put in the van, they're first out. Be careful none of your stuff accidentally makes it onto the forest floor if you plan on leaving it behind.

Mid-task, bring up a gripe, laying it on thick just how much they annoy you. Wait for their response — it'll usually be a rebuttal, them denying it, or, to deflect blame, they'll turn it around so you're the one getting it in the earhole.

You get angry. This is where your tools of the trade come in, and they're right on your body. First, you need to grab your mask from the back of the van and put it on. While your companion stands there wondering why the fuck you're wearing it, dig your thumbs into their eyes, using your fingers to hold the back of their head.

BONUS TIP: Latex gloves are great for getting a good grip.

Your target will thrash about and attempt to pull your hands away by grasping your wrists. This is where the knee comes in. Your neighbour doesn't have to be male for this to hurt. It's just as painful for a woman to be whacked where their hairy garden grows. Strike with all your might, ensuring you're ready to go down with them — keeping those thumbs and fingers in place. On the ground, straddle them, and dig, dig, dig into those juicy eye sockets.

As mentioned above, you'll need your wits.

Next, place your hands around their neck, making sure the heels press against their Adam's apple. Squeeze. Think of it as a giant tube of toothpaste. The wits come into play when your subject bucks and flounders. You need to be on the ball. It's almost like being on one of those bull-riding things, isn't it, except your victim is slapping at the mask, then again clamping on your wrists in an attempt to yank your hands away.

Neighbours. So pesky.

This process could go on for quite some time, so be prepared to become tired. But you mustn't let up. Keep strangling them until they cease moving. Now take your hands off. Wait ten minutes — you need to be certain they're actually dead, love. No reanimated corpses here. Simply not cricket.

Now it's time to sort the junk and decide what to do with it.

Claire had her very own scenario, a way to kill him without a weapon. Unless you counted her thumbs, knees and hands. Whether she'd be able to carry it out with her arms weakened and hurting the way they were, with her faint from hunger and thirst . . . well, she'd just have to see.

Now all she had to do was persuade him to untie her wrists and ankles.

Offer for him to touch her skin.

* * *

Andrew, in just Claire's holly knickers, pranced around his garden, doing the dance routine for the play. It didn't matter that he wouldn't be in it now — no one was available to direct it, and he hadn't gone back to the community centre since the night he'd taken Stacey. They knew him only as George, and it was better to keep it that way, put distance between them all, so he was forgotten, no one of consequence, just some smelly weirdo they used to know.

It was strange without Claire in her garden, reading while he practised. He couldn't jump over there to talk to her afterwards, but there was always Ginny, who hung her washing out now, putting her knickers on one of those pegs circle wotsits.

Wrong hair colour.

Not Ginny then.

Banging echoed, and he paused, cocking his head to listen.

Someone was making a racket out the front.

He went inside to peer through the living room window. A man carried a door up Claire's path, and another hammered in a new frame. As though she would be coming back. As though she'd open it of a morning, taking one of the many parcels inside containing a new handbag.

If only they knew she'd never darken that doorway again.

CHAPTER FIFTEEN

Andrew stood in the loft, on a beam, perched there hoping he wouldn't fall through the yellow fluff. She'd told him if he stepped on that, he'd go right through into the bedroom below. Do himself some damage. Most times, she did things so he jumped in fright, and she'd said it was so he might tumble onto the fluff. Plummet. Hurt himself.

She enjoyed seeing fear playing out on his face.

A bare bulb spewed minimal light, the wattage too low to be of much use, the flex short, cobwebs tangled around it, spun by spiders on instinct, although no flies would be caught in it. Not up here in the stifling attic, in a house on the outskirts of Shadwell, remote, where the early evening sun baked the roof and heat transferred inside. Everything had a gloomy appearance, those stacked boxes, old suitcases battered on the corners, a bird cage with a scattering of seeds on the bottom, an ancient exercise bike, kettle, crate of chipped cups, so many, many things she didn't want anymore, but didn't have the heart to throw away.

She had a heart for some things, just not him.

His sister, Dalene, didn't have to come here. Didn't want to perform. Andrew hadn't wanted to come anymore either after he knew what he was really here for, but his thirst for acting and dancing meant he arrived every week, six o'clock on the dot. Mother wouldn't hear of him giving up now. He had talent, she'd said. He'd be a star, someone for her to brag about.

Miss Estera Zabek lived here, performing arts teacher by day at the posh school down the road, the same profession by night but with an added lesson. Skin. She loved it. Yearned for it. Craved the touch of it from little boys.

She'd told him how it was the closest thing to a person. How someone letting their skin touch yours was an honour. It hadn't been at first. Just uncomfortable. Embarrassing. Especially when she was the one pressing her naked body to his.

They climbed up here once the first hour of acting lessons was over. This second hour . . . he wasn't to tell anyone about it. If he did, she'd come and kill his mum, but first, she'd burn the skin she most coveted and take it away from him.

He believed she would.

He'd been attending these lessons for five years now. How was he ten already? Where had the time gone? How had those years moulded him from a frightened child into one who craved skin as much as Miss Zabek? How had she turned him from pitiful and mistrusting to brave and devious?

"You're a replica of me," she said, pirouetting on a beam, her gold-spun hair dull in the meagre light.

She moved backwards, out of the light, and became a silhouette.

He wished she'd lose her balance and fall through the yellow fluff. Then he wouldn't have to come here. Wouldn't have to worry about her threats of breaking into the house at night and sneaking to his room to burn him and remove his skin.

When he was a man, he'd have an empty loft. Nothing but fluff in it.

"Time to undress," she said.

He stood, able to do so now without losing his footing, and took off his clothes. She beckoned him over, to the only part where wooden boards created a floor. She removed her dress, revealing pretty bronze-coloured knickers beneath, no bra, and again, when he was a man, he'd own knickers like that.

Miss Estera Zabek knelt, set the mechanical egg timer to half an hour. He stood in front of her, no need to be told, presenting his back, as always. She rested her skin to his and hummed, and he closed his eyes, understanding her need — it had become his now, that desire for touch, for the honour.

While the egg timer tick-tick-ticked, he thought about being on stage, the costumes, the old-fashioned shoes. The songs, the script, the dance moves. He imagined one day being a male version of Miss Zabek, forcing someone to stand behind him while they rubbed themselves against him.

While with her, he had accidents. In his pants. Ashamed, he washed them himself, scrubbing them in the bathroom sink to rid them of the stains so Mum didn't know. She always asked what he'd done on any given week and what he did with his underwear after he'd been to that lovely Miss Zabek's, and why he washed them himself. He never did tell her, shrugging so she'd drop the subject, think it was a private thing he wanted to do. She never questioned it, and that soured Andrew's perception of her. He was saving her life by having Miss Zabek play the game of skin. If Mum had asked more questions about his pants, would he have told her?

No, he wouldn't, but still, she should have pressed the issue. That was what mothers were supposed to do.

And he never did tell her about the skin either.

He couldn't. Otherwise, he might not have any, and she'd be dead.

* * *

He continued with the lessons until he became the man with the fluff-only loft, Miss Zabek's stolen bronze knickers in his drawer, and one who let his pants remain dirty as a reminder of what he'd been through, why he was here now, with a plan firmly in place. He'd indulged Miss Zabek, letting her think she still controlled him. Until tonight.

They hadn't gone into the loft. Instead, she'd asked him to stay to dinner. With no mother alive to ask for permission and Dalene off living her best life in London because of what he'd told her about taking the bronze underwear, Andrew chose this night to teach Miss Zabek a lesson. To show her how it felt to be manipulated into being a whole new person compared to the one he would have been had she not touched and threatened him. His nights had been plagued by bad dreams since the day she'd told him that she'd take his skin. It meant he never slept for long. He was desperate for eight nonstop hours. For peace.

So he would take her skin instead.

In the dining room of her large home, full of Polish knickknacks and furniture from days gone by, along with the two mannequins standing guard either side of the window in their Victorian and renaissance dresses, they toasted, her champagne flutes filled with sparkling liquid.

"Here, please place your napkin on your lap and prepare to feast," she ordered.

"To skin!" they said and downed the lot.

Andrew held the flute up for more, and the flames from the fire stared back at him through the glass, the smoke writhing from the tops of the licking orange tongues seeming to float out of the flute.

She dashed that image away by filling it and said, "I want your skin. For always."

He knew what she meant. She'd said so often enough — she'd burn his skin until it peeled, and then she'd pick it off, dry it out, and paste it to something, an item she could keep close. In a locket, perhaps, or maybe on a picture of him on her bedside table.

Except he wouldn't be the one burning tonight.

"Let's touch," she said, rising, taking off her dress, and, as always, revealing only knickers. Silk this time. Blue with a ribbon bow on the front.

Those ribbons had become a fetish of his.

He got naked, she set the timer, and he let her press herself to his back. And there came the hum, low, her movements languid, her gyrating on him. He planted his feet firmly on her oriental rug so she didn't knock him forwards, waiting until the thirty minutes were up when she allowed herself sexual release.

At the point she'd reached no return, he spun round, grabbed the flute, and smashed the rim against the table. The jagged edges sliced into her torso, blood spurting, landing on his stomach, hot and wet and beautiful, and she opened her eyes. He'd pulled her out of her orgasm to stare at the person she'd groomed for too many years to count.

He reached for a steak knife on the table and stabbed her between the ribs, the serrated blade snagging on gristle and bone.

"You'll never have my skin," he said. "But I'll have yours."

He shoved her to the rug, sat on her, and held her arm over the roaring flames in the grate. She screamed, and he loved that sound along with seeing the burn take effect. Her skin bubbled, blistered, eventually became charred flesh, and once it was over, he forced her to struggle up the attic stairs, where he tied her to a wooden roof beam by her wrists. She hung there, feet dangling over the yellow fluff.

"If you manage to undo those knots, you'll fall right through into the bedroom below," he said. "Do yourself some damage."

Then he pocketed her keys, left here there, until her skin decided to peel.

* * *

He buried her in the woods, her flakes of skin safe in an envelope at home, the Victorian and renaissance dresses hanging in his wardrobe inside large plastic bags, the same kind he'd put Miss Zabek in — a present to himself, like the fruit baskets she'd received from grateful parents for teaching their children. He'd stuck a ribbon at the top. Bronze, like his favourite knickers.

He'd dug the ground deep enough to conceal her, but shallow enough for animals to come foraging. Eating the evidence once they'd chewed a hole in the plastic. If they were hungry enough, they'd manage it.

He'd burnt her oriental rug with her blood on it. Cleaned her home from top to bottom to get rid of his fingerprints, his hair, anything to do with him.

Ten days later, with growing concern from the school and the parents who'd booked private lessons for their children, the police were informed. Ten days! She was missing, and wasn't that just awful?

They didn't speak to him. After all, no one knew he'd kept up the lessons into adulthood — Mum had always paid in cash, so he'd done the same. They didn't know her skin was on his silhouette. On the floorplan map, outlined in silver pen. The silhouette was hers, which he'd drawn and then cut out from memory. So many years of seeing her shape in the loft, knowing it off by heart.

It was a replica of her. The one who had ruined him.

* * *

One day, he joined a troupe, eager to take up acting and dancing again. To live the dream he'd once had to tread the boards for and to become the star Mum wanted him to be.

Stacey Maxey had gold-spun hair and a silhouette the same as Miss Zabek.

Skin.

CHAPTER SIXTEEN

Bottoms Up Bistro was a cross between Costa and a trendy, upmarket café, but the prices were low and wouldn't break the majority of down-on-your-luck banks.

They ordered coffee, and while Mike went off to find a table, Bethany asked to see the manager. Thirty seconds later, a woman appeared, hair in a tight bun and a body that spoke of her dashing about all day without a moment to take a breather. Name badge: LISA DOLATOWSKI.

Bethany led her over to a quiet corner and produced her ID, keeping it low so the customers didn't get an eyeful and think something was up with the place, like the rats in the kitchen UB40 reggae tune. "No need to worry. We're here for a coffee but also a couple of questions. Firstly, do you have CCTV?"

"Not outside, but we do have a camera behind the counter that moves from side to side throughout the day."

"Brilliant. Do you still have footage from yesterday evening? I'm specifically interested in a blonde lady, then a man buying lasagne and chips a short while later."

"I wasn't here last night, otherwise I'd have been able to tell you. Memory like an elephant. I'll be back in a mo."

Bethany glanced around and spotted Mike. "I'll be sitting over there." She pointed and headed that way. Once seated, she took a sip of coffee. Bloody lush.

"Any luck?" Mike asked, adding sugar to his cup and pouring it from a skinny sachet.

"She's gone to search the computer for purchases of lasagne — it'll be easier to pinpoint on CCTV once she gets a time."

"Even if Phillips is on it, that doesn't mean anything." He gave her one of his looks: *We might have to drop our suspicions regarding him. There's this George bloke to consider now.*

"I know, but it confirms he was here, which is something. One less timeframe for us to check where he's concerned." She drank some more.

After a bit, Lisa came over. "I've found both purchases — they were the only lasagnes sold last night. Do you want the footage on a memory stick? I have a spare one you can have."

"Would you mind if we watched it here first?" Bethany asked.

"Fine by me. If you'd like to bring your drinks, we'll go into my office."

They followed her through a door, down a hallway, then into a room. While Lisa got working on the footage and finding the correct segment, Bethany accessed her emails on her phone. No contact from Presley, no messages from Fran or Leona, but there was an email from Isabelle titled: FLAME RESULTS.

She clicked to read.

Beth,

Good news. Aradul has played a blinder and pulled a double shift — I've promised him we'll go on a date after this; least I can do. Anyway, the hard film on the flames in the champagne glass at Helen's is . . . wait for it . . . skin. That skin belonged to an unknown — nothing in the database to match. So someone, somewhere, has had their skin used. Absolutely revolting, but at least we now know we're dealing with someone who has a penchant for the stuff.

When you left the tent earlier, Presley had a look beneath Stacey's dress. Stab wound to the torso again. Said he'll know more at the post-mortem. He's doing Helen's today, by the way.

An update of my teams:

Skeleton crew at the woods doing the final evidence checks now Stacey has been removed. Main focus is to see if anything is in the earth beneath where Stacey was placed, plus, with a second body being found there, we've got some bloke coming in to use this special equipment that detects bones and whatever. Best we make sure there aren't more victims there, eh?

The other crew has finished at Claire's and the park. I let her father know, first thing, that he could go round and get a new door fitted. Bloody terrible that he has to do it when it was us who broke it, but those are the rules.

I'm sifting through scene photos of Claire's/the park. I'll ping you if I spot anything.

Later tater, and if you're feeling anything like me, you're knackered, so get some coffee down you.

Izzy

"Here you go," Lisa said.

Bethany handed her phone to Mike so he could read the email, pointing at it so he got the gist of what she wanted him to do. At the desk, she looked at the monitor. Lisa pressed PLAY, and the camera slowly panned across the bistro, starting from the left.

"Stop, please," Bethany said.

Mike moved to stand beside her.

Claire sat at a table, reading a Kindle.

"Look at the window," she mouthed to Mike.

Andrew Phillips stared in. Dark jeans, a sweatshirt. At least he'd gone out in public in more than his pants.

"Okay, can you continue to play, please," Bethany asked.

Lisa clicked the mouse. The camera reached its farthest right-hand point then continued left, then stopped and moved right again. A few back and forths showed nothing but Claire reading and Andrew still staring inside. That in itself was creepy. There sat a woman, oblivious to the fact she was being watched. No one at the other tables appeared to be disturbed by his presence, and the people walking past outside didn't seem to bat an eyelid. Had it come to the point where minding your own business was employed at such a level that even if you saw someone being ultra-weird, you did nothing about it?

Five minutes passed of this same footage, with various changes from other customers either leaving or arriving and the waitress delivering food and drinks.

Claire's meal was placed in front of her. She'd eaten half of it when Andrew walked to the door and entered. Ordered his food. Went to Claire's table and spoke. Claire looked up, annoyed, and said something, then he sat. She shoved her Kindle into her bag and rose. Strutted out. She turned right.

Andrew remained.

Shit. He didn't follow her.

He finished his whole meal and drink, and stayed in the bistro for another half an hour to eat a pudding.

"Do you happen to remember what that drink and dessert was on the till?" Bethany asked Lisa.

"Yes. A treacle sponge and custard. He had a Pepsi."

"Thanks."

On screen, Andrew got up and exited. He veered left, the opposite way to Claire.

Damn it.

Maybe he hadn't done anything to her. Bethany had to confess she might have got it wrong. The time on the monitor fitted with his version of events — he'd stopped to talk to Mr Lutworth for an hour after leaving Bottoms Up, then played with a ball in the park.

Fuck's sake.

"Can you fast-forward it for me?" She'd had enough, and the day was still young. It felt like they'd done a whole shift, but that was an early start for you, messing with your head.

Lisa sorted the fast-forward. Bethany wanted the footage running for a bit in case Andrew reappeared and went right. When the time showed an hour later and he hadn't appeared again, she admitted defeat.

"Okay, if we can have that lot on a memory stick, that would be great," she said.

While Lisa copied it over, Mike gave Bethany her phone back and indicated she had a message.

> Fran: NICOLA HAS BEEN TO SEE THE FAMILY FRIEND WHO WAS SUPPOSED TO HAVE HER NAILS DONE BY HELEN ON THE MONDAY. NOTHING TO REPORT. SHE'S MORE A FRIEND OF FAY CHOWN. ONLY KNOWS HELEN VIA HAVING ACRYLICS PUT ON.

> Bethany. OKAY, THANKS. WE'VE BEEN TO SEE ROGER ELLIS AND LAURA MACDONALD, THEN WENT TO THE COMMUNITY CENTRE TO SPEAK TO A JEFFREY VELPS — RUN A CHECK ON HIM, PLEASE, AS WELL AS ROGER AND LAURA TO BE ON THE SAFE SIDE. WE'RE AT BOTTOMS UP BISTRO NOW — GOT FOOTAGE OF ANDREW PHILLIPS REMAINING THERE TO EAT WELL AFTER CLAIRE ELLIS LEFT. NEXT UP IS TIPS AND TALONS, THEN THE SHANK — CLAIRE GOES TO QUIZ NIGHT THERE. RITA MIGHT HAVE SOMETHING USEFUL FOR US. WE'LL COME BACK ONCE WE'RE DONE.

> Fran: OKAY.

With the memory stick in her pocket, Bethany thanked Lisa for her help and led the way from the office, back into the bistro. They popped their cups on the tray stacker and, outside, she scanned the street. Houses stood opposite, and uniform had already been down here late last night, asking if anyone had seen Claire.

No one had.

Bethany drove them to Tips and Talons, a long, narrow shop with a row of women sitting behind a seemingly never-ending counter, each of them working on customers' nails. They must rake in the cash. Falsies were big business.

They spoke to the manager, who was upset at the news that Stacey and Helen were dead. One by one, they quickly questioned the staff, and although they sometimes got together as a group after work for a quick drink, none of them were particularly close except for Stacey and Helen. If their phone records came through today, Fran and Leona could study them to find conversations between the deceased ladies. There might well be some information there that would give them a ray of hope — and the means to know who the hell had abducted, burnt and then killed them.

And dressed them in the weird clothes.

Feeling no better off for speaking to the girls in the nail bar, Bethany got back in the car, a bit stroppy. "Fuck's sake!" She slapped the steering wheel, then wished she hadn't. It bloody well hurt.

"Frustrating, isn't it?" Mike said.

"Too right. All we need now is for Rita to not have been working last night and we've got another dead end, because the Shank manager isn't usually much cop at remembering things."

She drove away, parking up outside the pub, wishing she wasn't on duty so she could neck a glass of wine and wait for all her troubles to float away on a cloud of alcohol-induced pleasantness. They left the car, and Bethany glanced at her watch.

"How the chuff can it be ten-thirty already?"

"Time flies and all that," Mike said.

She pushed the door open and made a beeline for Rita, who stood behind the bar putting coffee cups in a stack beside the self-service machine. Mike caught up, notebook and pen out, as usual.

"Hi, loves." Rita glanced between them. "Day off?"

"Afraid not."

"Ah . . ." Rita nodded knowingly.

"Were you working last night?" Bethany asked.

"I was indeed. What do you need to know?" Rita grabbed some sugars and added them to a plastic wicker bowl.

"Claire Ellis. Know her?"

"Yep. She's a regular on quiz night with Katy and Viv. They were all in last night."

Bethany's heart leapt. "From and until . . . ?"

"Claire arrived first, and we had a chat, then the other two turned up. It was before eight, because that's when the quiz starts. I couldn't tell you a specific time for any of them, but they left just before ten."

"You say you and Claire chatted. What about?"

Rita frowned. "Has that bloody Andrew been up to anything? She told me about him."

Andrew again . . . "What did she say?"

"That he stole her knickers, keeps climbing in her garden in his shitty underpants, and follows her places."

Bethany resisted shuddering. "How did she seem?"

"Pissed off because he'd interrupted her meal at the bistro. She left because he sat at her table."

"How was she throughout the evening?"

Rita shrugged. "Happy enough. I did keep an eye on her, I must say, because of what she'd told me. Can't you do something about him? He shouldn't be allowed to go round being weird to people like that."

"We will do." Bethany smiled. "Has anyone mentioned Claire to you today?"

"No. Why would they?"

"She was abducted last night."

"What?" Rita shrieked, then glanced about at the customers.

They all stared over.

"Fucking hell. Sorry." Rita lowered her voice. "Abducted? When?"

"She walked home alone as far as we can tell. Took a shortcut through the park. Someone grabbed her in her street, right outside her house."

"Bloody hell, that's awful. Is it him? Andrew?"

Bethany wasn't prepared to give the woman gossip. "His time is accounted for as far as we can tell."

"So who would have done it then?"

Bethany ignored that. "Do you know a Helen Chown?"

"Yes, she went missing, didn't she. I only saw her in here Sunday night."

A break at last? "What time?"

"Again, no idea, but she came alone, had a G & T, seemed to be waiting for someone. She got her phone out, must have sent a message, then left."

"How long was she here for?"

"I don't keep tabs as a rule, except in Claire's case. It was different because I worried that bloke might come in and hassle her. It was busy for a Sunday. I don't know, maybe twenty minutes?"

"Do you have CCTV?"

"No."

Bethany didn't roll her eyes. Instead, she smiled. "What about a Stacey Maxey. Do you know her?"

"Yes, Helen's friend. They come here together from time to time. Stacey also meets her sister here, Laura. Saturday nights. They sink a few, then leave."

"When was the last time you saw Helen and Stacey together?"

"Blimey, you're determined to exercise the old grey matter, aren't you." Rita tapped her head. "Oh, I don't bleedin' know. Recently. Maybe a fortnight ago."

"The day?"

"Probably a Wednesday. Wouldn't be Thursday as Stacey does the acting thing."

"Did you ever hear any of Helen's and Stacey's conversations?"

"No, they always sit over there in the corner. Look, everyone round here knows Helen is missing, and now with Claire . . . Seeing as you're asking questions, is something going on with Stacey?"

"She also went missing." Bethany wasn't going to go into further detail.

"Eff me!" Rita rasped. "Shit, hang on, got to serve someone."

"It's fine. We're going." Bethany drummed her nails on the bar top. "If you hear anything . . ."

"Yep, I'll ring you."

"Thanks."

Back in the car on the way to the station, Mike said, "I'm surprised there hasn't been gossip about Stacey also being missing."

"As far as I'm aware, she hasn't hit the news. Maybe that git at *The Shadwell Herald* is slacking." She thought about Peter Uxbridge and wondered whether they should go to see him. He might know more than he'd reported about Helen. On second thought . . . He was such an arsehole, she'd rather avoid him. She'd get Fran to ring him instead.

"Unusual for him not to sniff out a story," Mike said.

"Hmm. Can you message Fran. Ask her to speak to Peter, see if she can get anything out of him. Also get her to look for a Katy and Viv."

"Yep."

"Tell her to go and see them, the women, or if she's strapped for time, ring them. We ought to go and bug Andrew Phillips again."

"Lovely," Mike said. "Wonder if he'll actually have clothes on this time."

CHAPTER SEVENTEEN

Two men worked at fixing on a new door. Bethany wondered whether Claire would ever get to see it, and her heart sat heavy. She'd knocked on Andrew's, and it seemed minutes had passed when it opened. He stood there, once more in filthy underpants. A skitter of disgust rippled up her spine. She gave him a warm smile, though, not wanting to raise his guard — also not wanting to give the workers a reason to earwig.

"Hi, so sorry to bother you again, but can we come in?" She jerked her head at Claire's door. Leant in and said quietly, "Wouldn't want to ask questions when we have an audience."

He nodded and stepped back, once again happy for them to go in. Was she barking up the wrong tree here with him? Bethany and Mike entered, and she had a good nose into the living room. Ancient furniture and a lot of foreign-looking ornaments. Nothing modern at all. Immediately, the Victorian and renaissance dresses came to mind — *someone who likes old-fashioned things . . .*

She coughed to get Mike's attention and pointed at the room. He glanced in then looked at her, nodding. Of course, he'd seen it before when he'd done a quick search. He obviously hadn't found it odd or he'd have said something.

They moved on to the kitchen, where Andrew stood leaning against an unfashionable pine sink unit, arms crossed over his skinny belly.

"Have you found Claire?" he asked, all concern, his eyes full of it.

"Not at present, I'm afraid," she said, unprepared to give him any more than that. "That's sort of why we're here. How are you coping with it all?"

"It's very sad," he said, sticking out his bottom lip.

He'd done that before. Maybe it was just a thing of his.

A silver whistling kettle sat on a range-type cooker and let out a shrill squeal as well as puffs of steam. The sound of water boiling bubbled, and the kettle rattled as if it might explode.

Bloody hell! Give me an electric one any day.

"Would you like some tea?" Andrew cocked his head.

The whistle trilled on. Got on Bethany's tits.

"No, thank you. We're not staying long," she said. "Just need to clear something up. All your alibis have checked out, so that's fine, but there's a space of time you can't account for. Can you move that kettle off the heat, please?"

He did, using a material pad.

Bethany carried on. "You said you were here, but we have no one to corroborate that. Are you sure someone didn't see you enter the house after you played football? Christ . . ." She rubbed her forehead for effect. "What time was that again?"

"I'm not sure," he said. "Nine, nine-thirty."

Her phone rang. She ignored it. "Ah, that's right. And you didn't go out again, you said."

"No. I was here when you came round, so you know I didn't."

"But you didn't answer when one of our officers knocked, and that's what's concerning me."

"I was in bed."

"Okay. Thanks for speaking to us again. We appreciate it."

He didn't seem flustered, just stood there holding the kettle midair.

"Why aren't you ever dressed?" she asked.

"I don't like clothes." Steam wiggled through the holes in the spout, and he blinked.

Doesn't like clothes? What? "I see." Although she didn't. "So what do you wear when you go out?"

"Oh, I wear them then." Pause. "But I don't like it."

"Maybe you need to live somewhere with a naturist camp nearby." She laughed, and it sounded false. Then she rushed on to drop her bombshell. "All that *skin* on show."

Like before when they'd been here, he didn't show any reaction.

He raised the kettle. "Are you sure you don't want tea? I've got Yorkshire. Nice, that is. The best tea."

She declined a second time and walked out. Mike closed the front door behind them, and she leant over the dividing garden wall and showed the workmen her ID.

"Has he been out today, do you know?" she asked, jabbing a thumb over her shoulder at Andrew's house.

"No idea, love." One man shrugged.

"Okay, thanks."

On the way to the station, she pondered Andrew: his furniture, the old kettle, the general feel of stepping back in time once they'd crossed the threshold. Him not liking clothes — was that normal or something that should concern them? Were there a lot of people who secretly paraded around their homes with just underwear on? She had no idea about that sort of thing, seeing as though she liked clothes herself.

Chuffing oddball.

"I still think he's strange," she said.

"He is, but strange doesn't mean he's a murderer."

"No, it doesn't."

She parked up, and they went inside, straight to the incident room. Bethany was flagging and needed a rest, but that wasn't in her future.

"Hi, you two," she said to Fran and Leona. "Got anything for us?"

Fran nodded. "I spoke to Peter Uxbridge. He said he doesn't know anything, although that's probably bullshit, knowing him. I found Katy's and Viv's surnames via Facebook, then ran them through a search. I phoned them — too much to do here for me to be gallivanting off visiting them. Both told the same story: they went to the Shank for quiz night and Claire walked home by herself like she always does. Claire seemed happy enough. They were devastated when I told them she was missing, and both said that although Andrew Phillips is weird, they didn't think he meant any harm. He's just got a crush on her, and Katy reckons it's sweet."

Sweet? Is she off her rocker?

"Right . . . We've just been to see Phillips, and yes, he's weird, but sweet isn't a word I'd use to describe him. There's something up with him." Bethany filled them in on everything they'd discovered this morning. "What about you two?"

"We've had the information back on sales of Victorian and renaissance dresses," Fran said. "Nothing in Shadwell recently, although a few months back, one similar to what Helen was wearing was sent to Stacey's address. I gave the community centre caretaker a ring, a . . . Jeffrey Velps, that's it, and he said the outfits for the play are stored in a box beneath the stage. He offered to go and see if they're still there. I asked him to wait and not touch anything. Glen went there and confirmed with Mr Velps that the outfits are all present, so the victims' dresses have come from elsewhere. No sales of boots to Shadwell, nor the velvet bags. As for ballerina shoes . . . They're popular. We're looking for a needle in a haystack there."

"Bumholes to it," Bethany said, walking to the whiteboards and adding information from this morning.

Everyone remained quiet while she did this, and she was grateful for that. She was tired and finding it difficult to concentrate, and she was likely to get ratty before the day was out. Once done, she accepted a coffee Mike had made then sat on the edge of Fran's desk. Her aching legs thanked her for it.

"Ooh, I've just had transcripts through from digi," Leona called out. "From the Books & Bags group Claire runs. It's from earlier today."

"Okay, print them out so we all get a copy and can read at the same time." Bethany's stomach rolled over. Would they get a clue now? More on Andrew? Something they could use to bring him in, question him, then catch him out regarding Claire?

The printer whirred, and Bethany moved over there. She took the copies out of the tray and handed them round. Perching on Mike's desk this time, she read.

> Fiona Hunt: Hi, all. Sorry to come off as a worry wart, but I've been thinking about Claire and that horrible neighbour of hers. She's usually chatting by now, but there are no comments or new posts from her since she said she was going out for dinner and then to a quiz night. Has anyone heard from her privately? I'm so worried he's gone too far and done something to her. She's said before that her family doesn't always speak to her every day, and didn't she mention her brother was away on holiday with his wife? Would anyone even know if something was wrong?
>
> > Liz Sutton: What's this about a neighbour? I wasn't online yesterday so must have missed it.
>
> Melanie Atkins: Liz Sutton A bloody weirdo, that's what. [HANDS ON HORRIFIED FACE EMOJI] Scroll down the main page and read. Fiona Hunt You've got me worried now. You're right. Claire's always chatting throughout the day. I'll go and message her.

Li Jayne: Oh God. I saw her post about him and got sidetracked so didn't answer. I was making the dinner [SAD EMOJI]

Leslie Mills: Maybe she's gone out to sort a camera and a new fence? [PRAYING HANDS]

Melanie Atkins: Leslie Mills She might have. I've just written to her on Messenger. No answer yet.

Fiona Hunt: I've got a bad feeling about this.

Liz Sutton: I've just read her post. Knickers? Dirty pants? What the hell?

Li Jayne: Liz Sutton Gross, isn't it?

Michelle Atkinson: Sod just sitting here. I'm going to call the police. Anyone have her address from the book exchange parcels?

Emma Smart: Michelle Atkinson I do. I'll DM it to you.

Michelle Atkinson: Emma Smart [LOVE HEART EMOJI]

Bethany rang Rob on the front desk. "Anyone call in about Claire Ellis? Someone from an online Facebook group?"

"They did," Rob said. "I tried ringing you earlier, but you didn't answer."

"Shit, sorry, we were with Andrew Phillips, and I forgot to check it once we got in the car."

"I emailed you the convo. Told her we're aware of Claire and not to worry."

"Thanks." She ended the call and brought up her emails. Read the one from Rob. To her team, she said, "Okay, a

Michelle Atkinson gave us a ring, stating her concern. Rob told her he'd get someone to ring her, so can you do that, Fran? I'm sending you the email with her details on it now. Like Rob did, tell her not to worry. The last thing we need is this getting out online. I'm so surprised it hasn't hit the news."

"Um, it has. Went online about fifteen minutes ago," Mike said, pointing at his monitor.

"Oh, for fuck's sake. Don't tell me, *The Shadwell Herald*, byline Peter fucking Uxbridge."

"You almost got it right," he said. "Take the 'fucking' away, and you're spot on."

"Sod off." She walked over to his desk to read.

"Did you just say Uxbridge?" Fran asked. "That git told me he didn't have any information."

LOCAL WOMAN ABDUCTED — THIRD INSIDE A FORTNIGHT!
TWO DEAD BODIES IN WOODS — WILL CLAIRE ELLIS BE NUMBER THREE?

PETER UXBRIDGE — REGIONAL CRIME

Shadwell resident, Claire Ellis, was abducted last night from outside her home. A neighbour reported hearing a shout and went outside to see Miss Ellis being hauled down the street and into the park. A source close to the investigation confirmed it's possible Miss Ellis was originally followed through the park where she lost one of her shoes. She made it into her street. There, she was attacked. Blood was at the scene. Then her pursuer vanished with her.

Is this connected to Helen Chown's disappearance? Her body, along with that of Stacey Maxey, another missing woman, was discovered in the woods a mile or so from Shadwell Hill. The bodies were buried metres from each other and possibly twenty-four hours apart. Forensic officers are still at the scene, looking for more graves.

If anyone knows anything, please ring The Shadwell Herald, Crimestoppers, or Shadwell police.

"That fucker," Bethany said. "He's put us last as a point of contact and himself first. What an absolute tosser."

"I always say this, but don't let him get to you." Mike closed the browser. "I'm interested in knowing who this 'source' is who keeps giving out information on our cases."

"We'll discreetly look into that when we get a moment."

"I've got another chat from digi," Leona said. "They're printing now. This is the latest one, Books & Bags, caught five minutes ago."

Bethany got up to retrieve them and once again handed them around.

Michelle Atkinson: Okay, I phoned the police. The man said he's aware of Claire and not to worry, whatever that means.

Liz Sutton: Bloody hell! I've just nosed at her on the local news. She's gone missing! [SHOCKED EMOJI] [BROKEN HEART]

Romy Brown: OMG! What the hell is happening? I can't believe this!

Rosey Goodwin: I feel sick. What on earth must she be going through?

Liz Sutton: It says she was walking through the park, being followed, and someone attacked her outside her bloody house! Then they took her away. [CRYING EMOJI]

Karen Davies: I'm only just seeing this. OMG!

Kay Hutcherson: This is horrible. Where does she live?

Liz Sutton: Shadwell. She was taken last night. It doesn't say when. I'll pop the news link here.

"Right, keep an eye on those emails from digi in case we get more," Bethany said. "This group looks to me like a set of like-minded people who have become friends, nothing for us to worry about. The more Phillips is mentioned, though, the more I'm convinced it's him, but then when we see him, I change my mind. What the fuck can we bring him in on?"

"Being out in public in his pants?" Mike suggested.

"Not funny, matey. We'd need for someone to have seen him doing that after he'd been warned about it."

"But he opened his door to us like it."

"He's inside his own home. If he was naked, another matter entirely. It's too flimsy. We need to find out who this George Bernard Shaw bloke is as well. Anything on that, Leona?"

Fran was still on the phone to Michelle Atkinson and waved her pen about to get Leona's attention. Leona went to Fran's desk and picked up a pad.

"No record of this George fella," Leona said.

Fran put the phone down.

"So it's just a name this man has given himself?" Bethany turned and read the notes on the whiteboards. They were full of information, and the pictures of Helen, Stacey, and Claire gave her a lump in her throat. "Fuck!" she shouted. "We have to find this bastard."

How? Whoever it was had taken those three women and spirited them off somewhere, seemingly without being noticed for Stacey and Helen, but there was a witness for Claire. They'd burnt them, driven them to the woods, and buried them.

Where is Claire?

Not knowing was sending Bethany mad. She paced, trying to sort through her thoughts, pissed off she couldn't find a good enough reason to collect Phillips and bring him in.

"Does Phillips own a car?" she asked whoever.

"No," Leona said. "But he passed his test a few years ago. The last car he owned was in twenty-ten."

"Any news on that Ford on CCTV?"

"No."

"Bloody hell! Okay, back to Phillips. What else do we have on him?"

"The usual education. Lived in Shadwell all his life. Mother and father deceased. Sister, a Dalene Phillips, lives in London."

"Ring her. Ask about him. Make out we're concerned because his neighbour has gone missing and we don't know how he's taking it because they're friends. Anything to get something on him. Stick it on speakerphone. I'm not doing it because I'm riled up. Before you do, though, what did you get on Roger Ellis, Jeffrey Velps, and Laura MacDonald?"

Leona shrugged. "Nothing. All clean."

"Fran, how did the phone call go with the Facebook group woman, Michelle Atkinson?" Mike asked.

"She's well upset, as you can imagine, especially now she knows Claire's missing."

"Okay, Leona, ring this Dalene." Bethany grabbed her coffee to give her something to do with her hands.

Leona found Dalene Phillips' number and dialled. It rang four times.

"Hello?"

"Ah, hello. I'm DC Leona Clinton, and I'm making a courtesy call about your brother, Andrew."

"What about him?"

"Please don't worry. What I'm concerned about is his neighbour, the lady next door. She has gone missing and your brother is friends with her." Leona pulled a face at that: *Friends, my arse.*

Yeah, if you can call pinching knickers and stalking being friendly.

Dalene's sharp intake of breath came from the other end of the line.

Leona went on, "We're anxious about his state of mind while the neighbour is missing. Do you think he'll manage okay?"

"Manage okay?" Dalene echoed.

Bethany scribbled on Leona's pad. Leona nodded.

"Does Andrew have any mental health concerns? Only, he seemed . . . does he have any issues we should be aware of?"

"Look, I don't have anything to do with him anymore. I live in London now. I don't see him."

"That's not a problem, but if you could just let us know if he needs help in dealing with something like this."

"No," Dalene said. "I don't want to talk about him."

The connection went dead.

"What was that all about?" Bethany's temper rose even more. "Is it just me, or was that dodgy as eff?"

"Dodgy as eff," Fran said.

Murmurs from Leona and Mike.

"Right, I want him looked into again. One of you go there and question the neighbours. Actually, both of you go. If he's odd, I don't want you at risk." Bethany's phone rang. "So help me God . . ." She snatched it out of her pocket. Isabelle. "Yep."

"You're going to love me . . ." Isabelle said.

"What now?"

"Bones, my dear. Inside a plastic bag."

"In the woods?"

"Yes. Ten metres up from Stacey's grave. They've been uncovered by us, obviously, otherwise I wouldn't be telling you about the bag. Want to come down and have a gander?"

"No."

"Really?"

"I don't *want* to, but I will. Won't be long." She shoved the phone away. "Right, we have bones, so we're talking years here since the person was killed. Whoever this is has topped someone, possibly had a long break, then started up again for whatever reason. Get on with speaking to Phillips' neighbours. Find out anything and everything." She gestured for Mike to go with her. "And who the fuck is George? We need to find him. We needed to yesterday."

CHAPTER EIGHTEEN

Bethany hadn't expected to be back here, standing in yet another tent in woods that had kept dead bodies a secret, the trees standing guard, watching, with their leaves whispering: *Come and find the buried, they're here, waiting* . . . Hikers and dog walkers would have ignored it, thinking it was just the wind rustling the leaves. But actually, they'd have trampled over graves, with a skeleton and fresh cadavers beneath their weary feet.

The halogen highlighted an open plastic bag that didn't seem to have been affected by the passage of time. No wonder people got up in arms about the stuff if it took a few hundred years to actually break down. Bethany had read that somewhere, and she was still shocked by it.

SOCO did their thing outside the tent, and a couple worked inside, as usual on hands and knees, searching, hoping to find something, anything: *Please let evidence be there*.

A skeleton rested exactly as the body would have — arms down by the sides, legs together. With no flesh and skin, it was a stark reminder that everyone ended up this way unless they were cremated, a framework of bones, nothing to tell one from the next until you looked closely at the teeth or pelvises and saw they were different. Here, there were no hopes, dreams, regrets, love, laughter . . . all was gone now for this person. As dead as they were.

Something had chewed through the plastic. An animal years ago, close to the burial time? That would explain why not even small, dried-out amounts of meat had not remained, because the bag hadn't been kept intact. Bethany imagined the creature crawling inside it over a matter of days, feasting.

A velvet pouch, or what was left of it after the mud and rainwater had had a good go at degrading it, sat beside the right femur, close to the hand, as if the dead had been holding the drawstring. With the absence of an old-fashioned dress or any other clothing, it was clear this individual had been buried naked.

Why?

People used woods to dispose of people, so the likelihood of a first killer choosing this spot was feasible, another MO entirely. But with the plastic bag and velvet pouch? No, it was the same bastard who'd murdered the others. How come they'd had a break of years between kills? Or had they continued and disposed of bodies elsewhere?

A victim buried in earth took some eight to twelve years to decompose, hair a shorter span of two, maybe a bit more, and given that the corpse was inside the plastic bag, that could add time. What was the killer doing in the interval? Working? Had they moved away then returned? Had this kill been the only one they'd thought they'd do, but the urge had come back?

"We're going to have our equipment man check this whole stretch," Isabelle said, reaching her arm out to encompass the woods beyond the tent. "Let's hope no others turn up, eh?"

"You can say that again," Bethany said.

Isabelle opened her mouth to repeat herself, a cheeky glint in her eye.

Bethany held her gloved hand up. "I didn't mean it literally." She sighed in a good-natured way. "Is it okay to check for ID, given the state of that pouch?"

Isabelle nodded. "All the pictures have been taken. I'll pop it in an evidence box. If the remains of it disintegrate, it'll at least keep all the bits together." She used a scoop, much like a fish slice, to pick up the remnants. Once they were in the box, the largest piece of fabric crumbled it was that brittle. What had been inside it rolled to one side.

A metal dog identification barrel.

"Hmm," Isabelle said and screwed off the lid. "So she didn't have a driver's licence like the others?" She used tweezers to pull out something wrapped in more clear plastic, then opened it, taking out a tiny, rolled-up piece of paper, amazingly preserved. Again, using tweezers, two pairs now, she opened the paper. It was about the size of a quote in a fortune cookie. "Estera Zabek, typed out, and someone's drawn those masks that denote the stage. You know, one with a smile, one with a sad face."

She turned it round so they could see.

"So she acted?" Mike mused.

"That's the logical explanation, but you never know with these nutbags. It could mean something else. Happy and tragic, I don't know." Bethany took her phone out.

With Fran and Leona out talking to Andrew's neighbours, she messaged Rob the details and asked him to find a next of kin.

Phone away again, she said, "Is there any evidence of there being a ribbon or holly leaves?"

"If there was, it's long gone now. And if there wasn't, maybe something's changed since this kill — they might not have used them with this one." Isabelle sorted putting the dog barrel, paper, and plastic wrapper into evidence bags. "The holly might represent a memory later in life."

True. Time made changes, sent you down different paths. Who knew what this killer had experienced between murders?

"Did the crime scene photos show anything we missed?" Bethany asked. "You said you were checking them."

"I was until this call came in, and no, I've seen nothing so far. I've left a couple of my team sifting through them.

We took so many, so it's a mountain of a job to study each section of an image close up. As you know, it scoffs hours."

With two graves bar this one, plus Claire's house, her front garden, the wall and pavement, there was also the park. There had to be a thousand pictures at least.

"I don't envy them," Bethany said.

"Me neither, and I'm a wicked cow, but I'm kind of glad I'm here instead. Anyway, back to work . . . Looking at these ribs" — Isabelle pointed to the skeleton — "it seems to me like they were stabbed. There's a miniscule scrape on one of them. See it?"

"I don't fancy getting that close to it, thanks." Bethany smiled. "I'll take your word for it, though. So, this is another sign it's the same person. The stab is in a similar area." She used her protective suit sleeve to scratch her cheek. "What does this woman have to do with Helen, Stacey, and Claire?"

"Maybe nothing," Mike said. "But I'd put a bet on it she was blonde."

Bethany nodded. The pelvic bone was of a female. *Yet another link*. "We — Ooh, hang on." She checked her phone message.

> Rob: AN ESTERA ZABEK WAS REPORTED MISSING SEVERAL YEARS AGO. ORIGINALLY FROM POLAND. CAME OVER HERE TO TEACH PERFORMING ARTS AT THE PRIVATE SCHOOL, THE KING ARTHUR. SHE ALSO TAUGHT IN THE EVENINGS AT HOME. HER NEXT OF KIN IS PROBABLY STILL THE MOTHER, WHO IS DOWN IN OUR FILES BECAUSE A SMALL INVESTIGATION TOOK PLACE TO TRY TO LOCATE MISS ZABEK. MOTHER LIVES IN POLAND, ALTHOUGH THAT MIGHT HAVE CHANGED — OR SHE MIGHT BE DEAD. WILL KEEP DIGGING.

Bethany: THANKS, MUCH APPRECIATED. WHEN FRAN AND LEONA GET BACK, CAN YOU PASS THAT ON TO THEM? THEY'LL TAKE OVER FROM YOU.

Rob: WILL DO.

"Okay, so this lady here was a performing arts teacher," she told Mike and Isabelle. "That explains the acting masks."

"How lovely for you to have to go through all her contacts, if you can even find them now, track them down, and ask them questions when so many years have passed."

Bethany released a long breath. "This case just keeps getting better, doesn't it? Thankfully, there's a missing person's report on her, so a lot of her friends and whatever will be on there. We'd better get back and make a start on it."

They left Isabelle to it.

Seeing as lunchtime was creeping up on them, she drove to a Tesco Express and nipped inside to pick up some sandwiches in a meal deal. They ate while still parked, and it reminded Bethany of when Cuppa, Vinny's friend and colleague, had almost seen her another time they'd been stuffing their faces in the car like this ages ago. She'd avoided the poor man since her husband's funeral, and now, too many months had flown by for her to get hold of him, thank him for his texts where he'd asked her if she was okay.

Hadn't they?

Sod it, she was stronger now, more able to cope with condolences, and also had no trouble telling people she didn't want to talk. Grief was a hard task master, but it had taught Bethany to only deal with what she could handle.

Bethany: HEY, JUST A QUICK ONE TO SAY I APPRECIATED ALL YOUR MESSAGES. I DIDN'T GET BACK TO YOU BECAUSE EVERYTHING WAS TOO RAW. IT STILL

IS, BUT I DIDN'T WANT TO LEAVE IT ANY LONGER, SO HERE'S HOPING YOU AND YOURS ARE OKAY. YOU KNOW ME, TOO BUSY TO HAVE A MEGA CHAT, SO IF I DON'T REPLY, YOU'LL KNOW I'M UP TO THE EYEBALLS IN WORK OR JUST PLAIN DON'T WANT TO TALK IN DEPTH ABOUT VIN YET, PROBABLY NEVER WILL. ANYWAY, BIG HUGS, AND TAKE CARE. XXX

She hit SEND then pushed her mobile into her pocket. "I just texted Cuppa."

Mike smiled and reached over to pat her shoulder. "It all comes in due course, the moving on. Glad you did it. Even more glad you did it when *you* felt like it, without being pressured. You've had enough to deal with without being guilt-tripped into answering every bugger who got hold of you." He paused, held the corner of a crust up. "Nice sandwich, this."

God, she loved him for switching to another subject without making a song and dance about it. He seemed to understand her completely, and that was what brothers were for — and she saw him as a brother. After all they'd been through since Vinny had died, they may as well be siblings. Mike had seen her crying until she couldn't breathe, tended to her after nightmares, wiped her tears . . .

"You're my best mate, you know that?" she said.

"Yep, I know. And you're mine. I reckon that's going to be a bone of contention when we next get other halves, by the way."

"Was that a pun?"

"Eh?"

"Bone of contention. We've just seen a load of them . . ."

"For fuck's sake, no." He popped a blueberry in his mouth from the fruit pot he'd got as part of his meal deal.

"As for getting another half . . ." She scrunched her nose up. "I can't see me doing that for a long time, but if I do, and the bloke is iffy about you, well, he can just fuck off, can't he."

Mike laughed. "I can see you saying that an' all."

She tossed her sandwich carton in the back then opened her salt and vinegar McCoy's. "Shit." She dropped the bag in her lap to answer her phone, putting it on speaker so Mike could hear. "Yep."

"We're back from Phillips' street," Fran said. "Didn't take long. Hardly anyone was in — we assumed they're at work — and those who *were* at home just said about him sometimes being out the front in his pants. I asked if they'd seen him doing it recently, so we could bring him in on that, but he hasn't done it for a while. All in all, he's just a strange bloke they tend to steer clear of. I've managed to track his job history, but it's as though he works for a bit to get the benefit people off his back, then happens to lose it again so he can claim the dole. Well, Universal Credit now. He gets fifty-odd quid a week and his rent paid, plus his council tax. This bloke is forty, for God's sake, and doesn't appear to have any direction in his life at all."

Bethany told her who the skeleton used to be. "Did Rob give you that info?"

"Yes, he did. Leona's already made a start on it. I was thinking . . . Say the body took ten to fifteen years to decompose, if we're thinking of Phillips for this, he'd have been twenty-five to thirty when he killed this woman."

"So we need to find out whether he knew her. Surely there's a connection somewhere."

"Hang on. Let me pass you to Leona."

"Okay."

"Hi," Leona said. "I'm looking at the file on Estera Zabek, and her parents arranged to have all her belongings put into storage here in the UK, and they paid for it, probably in the hopes their daughter would come back, the poor sods. Anyway, I was wondering, should I contact her mother — or try to anyway — and ask her if she still rents the box?"

"Yes. Contact the Polish police. Actually, get Jakob from drugs to do it — he's Polish, isn't he? Saves buggering about with an interpreter. Get him to ask her if she'll give permission for us to view the stuff. Piddle. I've just had a thought. Jakob will have to tell her we think we've found her daughter's remains."

"I'll sort it, don't worry," Leona said.

"We're just about to come back now anyway," Bethany said. "Finishing our lunch first, though."

"Okay, see you in a bit."

Bethany slung her phone on the dash and turned to look at Mike. "We've still got twenty minutes left of our lunch break so may as well take it. We started work at the crack of dawn, so let's just have a breather."

She ate her crisps while Mike finished his fruit.

Her phone blipped.

> Cuppa: BLOODY HELL, BETH, IT WAS GREAT TO HEAR FROM YOU. YEP, ME AND MINE ARE ALL FINE. THANKS FOR CATCHING UP. AND YES, I DO KNOW YOU, SO I'LL LEAVE IT FOR YOU TO MESSAGE ME BACK WHENEVER. LOVE YA! XXX

Guilt jumped on her shoulders and clung on, heavy, gnawing. She showed Mike the message, a lump in her throat, tears burning. He raised his eyebrows, seeming to know exactly how she was feeling.

"Don't you dare feel bad," he said. "You did what you had to, to get through one of the worst things people have to deal with. It's all sorted now with Cuppa, so that's an end to it."

What would she do without this man?

"Shall we talk about something else?" she asked.

"I'll talk about whatever you want, you know that." He opened his bottle of Coke.

"I'm dreading going through all Zabek's contacts when we get back."

"Same here, but someone might remember something after all this time. Incidents like your friend or colleague going missing tend to stick in the mind, don't they."

Yet again, her phone went off.

Leona: THE MOTHER HAS GIVEN PERMISSION TO SEARCH THE STORAGE PLACE. SHE'S EMAILING THE MANAGER. YOU JUST HAVE TO TURN UP. OH, AND SHE WAS RESIGNED, KNEW HER DAUGHTER WAS DEAD BECAUSE OF THE NUMBER OF YEARS THAT'VE PASSED. SHE SAID SHE'LL BE COMING OVER NEXT WEEK TO SIFT THROUGH ZABEK'S BELONGINGS TO SEE IF THERE'S ANYTHING SHE WANTS TO KEEP. I'LL CHASE UP THE PEOPLE FROM ZABEK'S MISSING PERSON'S REPORT AND SEE WHERE THEY ALL ARE NOW. SHOULD HAVE THE LIST READY BY THE TIME YOU GET BACK.

Bethany: OKAY. ADDRESS FOR THE STORAGE FACILITY?

Leona: THE BIG RED BOX, HANDMILL STREET. HER STUFF IS IN SEVENTY-EIGHT.

Bethany: THANKS. TTFN.

She started the engine.

"Abandoning having a whole lunch break, are we?" Mike asked. "What a surprise."

"Yeah, reckon we ought to get to that storage place as soon as poss."

Once there, she grabbed her phone off the dash. They spoke to the manager, a Mr Swift, who showed them to Zabek's 'room' inside what was indeed a big red box, a warehouse. The place was a maze of corridors, and she reckoned they'd get lost on their way out if it wasn't for the arrows on the walls pointing the way to the exit. Swift left them to it, and Mike used the key. They stepped inside, and Bethany gasped.

Furniture similar to that in Phillips' house lined the edges, a birdcage standing out, and she had to remind herself that coincidences were real sometimes. However, some of the ornaments were the same, or very close to it, and it disturbed her.

"Are you seeing what I'm seeing?" she asked.

Mike nodded. "Unfortunately, furniture isn't a reason to bring him in."

"I know, but I bloody wish it was." She made a beeline for some cardboard boxes. In most of them were items wrapped in newspaper, and it took her a good hour to look inside them all to check what they were — cups, plates, things like that.

Mike was busy sorting through others, and he pulled out a box file. Placing it on a patch of dining table that wasn't covered by anything, he opened it. "Bills and the like." He lifted a wedge out and flicked through them. "Electricity, telephone. Ah, what's this . . ." A spiral-bound notebook sat halfway down the stack.

"Let's have a shufti then," she said.

Mike flipped the pages. A list of names, all stars of the stage or playwrights. Each one had a day of the week and a time beside them.

Greta Garbo. Mondays. Four p.m.
Ingrid Bergman. Mondays. Five-thirty p.m.
James Dean. Wednesdays. Five p.m. until seven.
Shakespeare. Thursdays. Four p.m. until six.

"So she gave them nicknames?" Bethany frowned.

"It was probably fun for the kids," Mike said.

She carried on reading the list.

George Bernard Shaw. Fridays. Six p.m. until eight.

"Shit a brick," Mike said, glancing up at Bethany.

She shook her head, trying to accept what she'd seen. "Who the hell *is* that?"

The final line chilled her, and she sucked in a breath.

James Dean, Shakespeare, George Bernard Shaw: Skin.

CHAPTER NINETEEN

Claire stared at Andrew, her stomach killing her from lack of food and her arm skin tight from where it had dried and was healing. Her saliva had disappeared ages ago, and her mouth and throat were so parched. She wouldn't ask him for water again, though. He hadn't liked that last time.

He'd walked in naked apart from her holly knickers. Sickened by the sight of his bulge *there*, she struggled to keep her eyes open. The lure to shut the image out was strong, but he'd told her to watch him. She'd have to obey and do whatever he said, if it meant getting on his good side.

"I'm going to serve you." He opened a Tesco carrier bag he'd placed on the crate. "This is a part I played once, where I was a butler. I hope you enjoy it. There will be so many plays I do for you."

So many? That meant he didn't intend to kill her.

Hope bloomed.

She almost groaned at having to see him acting. How many times had she had to suffer this when he'd pranced about in his back garden, waffling about George Bernard Shaw and the like? But if it meant a drink or food, she'd do whatever he said. *Whatever*. She needed to get her strength up to do what had to be done.

He turned and smiled at her. Sinister. Unsettling. "And then we're going to *skin*."

What does that even mean?

Her heart thudded hard for a few beats, then fluttered, palpitations that left her struggling to breathe, fear of not getting enough air adding to the ominous feeling slinking through her. Was he going to actually *skin* her?

He took out a bottle of water, a small silver tray, and a package of sushi. She hated that stuff, but it was food, and she was too hungry to be picky.

"If you skin with me, I won't burn you again." Head tilt.

I so hate you.

I'll skin with you, she said, silently, the words unable to be sounded out because of her dry throat. *I'll do any damn thing so long as I get out of here.*

He opened the sushi and water, then placed them on the tray. Raising it high, balancing it on his fingertips, he walked towards her, his bulge deflated now, lust a lump. She felt better about that. He wasn't . . . excited.

He knelt, lowering the tray. "Here. Please place your napkin on your lap and prepare to feast." He'd put on a silly accent, a foreign one, and it was high-pitched, like a woman.

Using his fingers — *Where have they been? Do I even care anymore?* — he offered her some rice and salmon wrapped inside that nasty green stuff. Seaweed? She opened her mouth and forced herself not to scoff it but instead go slow to give her stomach a chance to accept it. Her saliva was back again, flooding her mouth, easing the chew.

She swallowed. Eyed the water. And he gave her some, tipping the bottle.

It was the best thing she'd ever drunk.

"To skin!" he said, as though toasting.

Fucking hell, fucking hell . . .

More food came, and he alternated feeding her with sips of water. Her tummy didn't revolt, thank goodness, and he smiled at her, stroking the burns on her arms, the scabs rasping on his fingertips. She held back a scream — *so painful;*

please, stop doing that; God, I can't take this anymore — and smiled, as though she was loving every minute of it.

"It's not so bad, touching," he said. "Is it?"

It's evil. "No. It's good."

He nodded, slowly, as if he'd known she'd come round in the end. Then he undid the ropes, and she couldn't believe her luck. She'd have to play this right, like Scenario Eighteen. Do whatever he said, give him a false sense of security.

Then she'd strike.

* * *

CLAIRE'S SCENARIO

Necessity: Murder him and get the fuck away.

NEEDED:
THE WILL TO LIVE
THE URGE TO KILL
THE GUTS TO CONCEAL A MURDER

You're there, in your scenario, the one you've dreamt of for so long. And your neighbour, *he's* there, standing before you in just your Christmas knickers, the ones he stole and has done God knows what to since he took them. You think about that, so it helps build the rage you'll need, and that rage, it boils, swims through your veins until you think you'll burn from the inside out.

Your arms have scabbed over in places, but some parts are tender and wet with a yellow substance you can't bear to look at. The surrounding skin is scarlet, tomato red, still hot, still seeming to sear down through your muscles, into your bones.

But you'll do what you have to despite that. Despite the pain.

You have to. This is life or death. This is your life or his.

He pulls you to standing, his hands on yours, and the contact . . . you want to retch but hide it behind another smile, one where your face aches it's that forced.

"Stand over there." He points to the wall behind you.

You contemplate running, *now*, without hurting him for all the times he's hurt you, but the door is shut, and that will slow you down trying to open it with fumbling fingers.

Best to wait.

That's a voice in your head, the words of the side of you who wants to survive.

Take your time.

You suck in a deep breath and do as he says, so aware that you're naked. You bite back a scream, that stubbornness in you coming back — again, you don't want him to know you're in agony.

Sweat pops on your forehead.

He says, "You're not a silhouette."

You have no idea what the hell he's going on about, but it's got him angry, and you don't want that. He needs to be calm, trusting, relaxed.

"It'll have to do," he says, coming to stand in front of you.

Here's the perfect opportunity to use your thumbs, to jab them into his creepy-as-eff eyes, to knee him in the groin, have him doubling over, gasping. But you don't.

Wait. Wait . . .

"It's time to skin, Claire Bear."

He turns his back to you, presses himself against your front, and my God, this is hideous, shudder-inducing. Your skin touches, breasts squashed by his shoulder blades, and he shivers.

"Hum," he says.

What?

"Hum!" he repeats.

And you do.

Miss Polly had a dolly who was sick, sick, sick.

He's sick. And he'll be your dolly to do with as you please. Soon.

"Rub on me," he says.

Oh God. This has gone further than you'd like. In a direction you dread.

So she called for the doctor to come quick, quick, quick.

But you do as he wants, moving against him, shutting your mind off as to what you're doing, pretending it isn't happening. Pretending you're at home or on a beach somewhere, not here, with him, with this monster.

"That's it," he says. "Just . . . like . . . that."

Tears burn your eyes. You remember him rubbing his body on the garden fence. Revulsion sears up your windpipe in the form of bile. The sushi, the water, they're threatening to come out, but you carry on, swallowing, telling yourself it'll be over soon.

The doctor came with his bag and his hat, and he knocked on the door with a rat-a-tat-tat . . .

If only someone would knock on the door now. You could wait for him to answer it, then scream, shout for help. Rush out there and let the person see you, the state of you.

"Breathe heavy," he demands. "Like you're enjoying *skin*, Claire. Get off on this."

That's it. You can't stand it anymore.

You lift your arms, slowly, knowing you're the wrong way round for this, that you can't use your thumbs like Scenario Eighteen. But you slap your palms on his temples, dig those thumbs into the back of his head, and curl your fingers. The tips meet with closed eyelids, but you press anyway, and there, so beautiful, so wonderful, is the wetness you've craved, your fingers sinking into his sockets, his eyes a pressure you push and push.

Just like in *One Hundred Ways to Kill Thy Neighbour,* he raises his hands to grasp your wrists. Shouts. The next best thing to kneeing him in the dick is to do it in his tailbone, so you move back, still grabbing his head, and land a hard blow. He bends forward — *oomph* — taking you with him, and you're curled over his back, a limpet, refusing to let go as he staggers around.

No more humming. Instead, you screech with rage.

He drops to the floor, and you're both fighting to be the one in charge. You lose your grip, and he's on you in a second, straddling, resting on top, his bulge against your . . .

No. No . . .

His eyes, they're bleeding, swelling, the whites a vivid bright red. You weave your hands between you, rest your palms to his chest, and absently register some of your arm scabs cracking. Your temper means you don't feel the pain of it, and you shove him, hard, creating space, then use all your might to give one more monumental effort in getting him the hell off you.

He lurches to the side, and you scramble up, on your feet now, and kick him in the face. Keep kicking, that's it, give him what he deserves. But he grabs your ankle, tugs, and you go back down there, with him, too close — so close his breath fans your cheek.

You reach across for the tool, the one that so cruelly burnt you, and switch it on. He stares at the blue-turquoise flame and makes a grab for the handle, but you bring that heat down, pointing it into his face.

He shrieks, his hands automatically going to his cheeks, and you manoeuvre a bit so you're on your knees. The back of his hand is turning yellow, the skin lifting.

"Watch how it rises in a pretty bubble," you say, giving his earlier words back to him. "Fascinating."

Then you concentrate the blue heat on his eye, cooking it, roasting, watching as it shrivels up while he screams and claws and bucks and writhes.

"Is that hurting badly?" you ask and keep burning until his flesh chars, his cheekbone showing through, and he flops onto his back.

Next, the Sharpie is in your hand, and you jab it into his neck, right where it needs to be.

You think of the technicalities, how they matter this time, because this isn't a fantasy, it's real. You've killed a man, and while you've imagined it so many times, the reality of it unfurls inside you, warning you that this can't be covered up.

Can it?

* * *

Claire dragged her clothes on, tears of relief and terror and determination hot on her cheeks. She left him there, rushing out of the room to find what she needed.

Remember Scenario Four . . .

They must have been in what was once a lounge, as a kitchen was the only other room on this floor. And there it was, the gift from karma, beneath the sink, a pile of old newspapers. The front page of the top one had a disturbing headline: POLISH TEACHER GOES MISSING. She grabbed the stack and took them into the lounge, where Andrew was still dead, and she laughed, pleased he hadn't got up, ready to touch her again. After dumping the newspapers on the floor, she scouted the rest of the house.

Scenario Four's advice: *Collect as many things as you can.*

In one of the bedrooms, a broken chest of drawers lurched to one side, and she hefted it with all her strength to the top of the stairs, then pushed it down. On the way to the bottom, it fell part, landing in bits, one of the knobs flying off and smacking into the wall. She did the same with a single divan bed base, and while it didn't break, it didn't matter. Next was a bookshelf, covered in dust and cobwebs.

You can do this. You have to.

She went down and clambered over the furniture, scraping her inner thigh on an exposed screw. She dragged each piece into the lounge. Placed them all around him. Threw the newspapers everywhere, laughing, giddy, each page separating to float then land in random places, one of them over his wrecked face. She glanced around at the crumbling walls, the beams on the ceiling, the flimsy windowsill, the wooden back door. Grabbed her handbag, her Kindle. Then picked up the tool. Switched it on.

And set the fucking lot alight.

* * *

CLAIRE'S SCENARIO

Necessity: Lie until you believe it.

NEEDED:
THE WILL TO STAY OUT OF PRISON
THE URGE TO ENSURE YOU GET AWAY WITH THIS
THE GUTS TO FABRICATE A STORY FOR THE POLICE

You walk out of that house, into the little front courtyard, and turn to face the building. Look inside, down the hallway. Flames have crept to the lounge door already, devouring, climbing up the frame, snapping and crackling. You imagine *him* inside, his body being deliciously cremated, and you think: *Now you know how skin burns, Andrew.*

You cover your hand with the hem of your black sparkly top and grasp the knob, close the door, face away from that awful scene and check your surroundings. There's a car parked close, and it brings back memories of you inside the boot, fighting to break that backlight, hoping someone would hear you kicking the interior. And this place, it's in the middle of nowhere, in a field overgrown with long grass and weeds that stretch on and on, and you tell yourself that even though you have no shoes on, you have to walk. You recall the trees behind the house, the tiny houses, and wonder if you should head that way, but there's the road ahead, and that's the one you need to take.

You reach it, and it's so quiet, as though no one ever uses it, a backwoods area lost to humanity. And that suits you. Less chance of anyone seeing the fire, except you'd heard cars on a road out the back, by the houses, so someone will be close by at some point. And, of course, the smoke will tell the story, perhaps visible for miles. You glance over your shoulder, and, quicker than you thought it would, that fire has taken hold. The windows have orange tongues licking the panes, even upstairs, and the first black tendrils sneak through the broken tiles on the roof, sharing your secret.

You recall him turning left onto the property when he'd brought you here, so you veer right, and it'll take you back to Shadwell. The random bits of grit on the tarmac bite into the soles of your feet, but you've endured worse than that. Your arms throb as testament to the torture he put you through, but the spring air seems to soothe them somehow as you roll the sleeves up as high as you can. Your heart aches with the terror he inflicted before he'd taken you, little ripples of fear undulating in your chest. Your head is filled with wretched memories — his face, his pants, his everything.

You'll never forget.

Home calls, so loudly, so insistent, but you tell yourself you can't go there. Not yet. There's something else you must do first. You switch your Kindle on to find comfort in reading while you head towards freedom.

Thirty-five percent.

And you smile at that.

You made it out before the battery went dead.

CHAPTER TWENTY

With SOCO down at The Big Red Box busy bagging and tagging all of Estera Zabek's belongings, and a picture of the list in the notebook on Bethany's phone, she stood in front of the whiteboard and added the new information. They'd arrived back at the station around three, and a team meeting was in progress, Chief Kribbs included, to get everyone up to speed. The majority of the points had been addressed, so the main thing on the agenda was finding George Bernard Shaw.

"Okay, Fran, Leona, hit us with what you've got from speaking to the people listed in Zabek's file at the time she was reported missing."

Fran grabbed her A4 pad. "Right, there were a few parents of children having Zabek's lessons, and they're stumped as to what happened to her. However, there are some from the past who came forward, where the children were adults at the time of her disappearance. Maybe they felt compelled to ring us because they'd been associated with her at some point in the past; they didn't elaborate on that. So, I've established who the following are: Greta Garbo, Ingrid Bergman, James Dean, Shakespeare. I'll stick to those names for now, so it doesn't get confusing. Based on James and Shakespeare having 'skin' mentioned, I pressed the men in question as to what that means, and Shakespeare doesn't want to 'dredge up the past'. I pushed him pretty forcefully, explained this is a murder investigation, and he's standing firm in not revealing what happened. James, however, is on his way down here now to give us a statement."

"Brilliant," Bethany said. "I'm curious as to what the hell went on back then."

Fran continued. "The women, Greta and Ingrid, sounded stumped about 'skin', and I believed them and think we're dealing with a female teacher who did whatever she did with young male students."

Bethany's heart sank. "Sexual abuse?"

Mike winced. "I bloody hope not. Those poor lads."

Kribbs rubbed his forehead. "It's a good job she's dead, otherwise we'd all want to string her up if that's the case."

"So no mention of George?" Bethany asked. "No parent ringing us?"

"No," Leona said, "but don't forget, we'll have to go through all Zabek's paperwork, her bank statements, so maybe something will crop up there."

"Unless the parent paid in cash." Mike sighed.

"That'd be just our luck," Leona said.

Bethany's mobile rang. Rob. "Hi."

"A man by the name of Ian Oliveson to see you. Said you'd know him as James Dean."

"Ah, okay. Down in a sec."

Bethany told the team he'd arrived, then she and Mike went downstairs. A man of around forty stood by the front desk, a woman beside him, older, his mother, going by the facial resemblance. She'd been crying, that much was obvious, her eyes red and glassy.

In the soft interview room, with the video running, she smiled and explained how this would go. Ian nodded on the sofa, and his mother, Hattie, clutched his hand, pressing herself into his side. They appeared tight-knit, close.

"What were your sessions like with Miss Zabek at first?" Bethany asked, thinking it best to start from the beginning.

Ian shuddered. "She was nice. Didn't start that skin lark until I'd been there a couple of months and she'd got my trust."

"Do you want to go straight to what happened?"

He nodded. "She told me when people let another person touch their skin, it's an honour. I didn't quite get it, as I was only about ten, wasn't I, so I didn't answer her. She said, 'Do you want the honour of touching my skin?' I didn't, to be honest, but she said if I refused to let her 'skin' with me, she'd make sure my mum got hurt. Oh, and she added that no one would believe me if I told on her anyway." He shrugged, but not a gesture of him not caring, more of resignation. "I was a kid, she was an adult, and I believed everything she said."

Hattie whimpered. "I wish you'd told me."

"I didn't want you hurt, Mum."

"It was just a threat," Hattie said. "Something to get you to keep your mouth shut."

"I know that now, but at the time . . ." He closed his eyes for a moment. "She took me up into her loft, tied my wrists to a roof beam, and made me stand on another. She kept saying that if I stood on the insulation fluff, I'd fall through and die. So I . . . so I stayed still. She got undressed, then untied me, and she used this egg timer, setting it for thirty minutes. And put me in front of her and . . . oh God . . ."

"Take your time," Bethany said, disgusted by this story.

"She made me take my clothes off and rubbed herself against my back."

More came, harrowing, depraved, revolting stuff that no adult should do to a child and no child should endure. It was obvious what Zabek gained from the encounters, and with three little boys at her disposal, she got her kicks frequently. If George had killed her, Bethany could see why. Maybe his head was so full of rancid memories he couldn't stand it anymore. He'd murdered her, buried her, and put the past to bed. But something must have triggered him recently. Maybe the blonde hair, something Stacey or Helen had said to him had set him off, and he'd been transported back to the past.

"Do you know who George Bernard Shaw was — as in, a student of hers, not the real man?"

"No."

They continued talking, and after Ian had finished his statement, and with no one to bring to justice for the crime of sexual abuse, what with Zabek being dead, Bethany could do nothing but offer him a list of therapists for counselling.

"No," Ian said. "I've dealt with it in my own way over the years. I've got a lovely wife who knows everything — sorry, Mum."

Hattie patted his hand. "It's okay."

Mother and son left, off to patch up their lives as best they could now the horrors had come out into the open. Bethany couldn't allow herself to think about the hell Ian's life had been, and Shakespeare . . . he'd undoubtedly suffered the same. No wonder he hadn't wanted to dredge it all up. She messaged Leona for counselling phone numbers to be sent to him, too.

Bethany and Mike remained in the interview room, staring into space, absorbing Ian's tale. Her phone jangled and, wearily, she took it out of her pocket.

Fran.

"Hey, you."

"Sorry to interrupt," Fran said, "but you really need to hear this. Jakob just rang me. He spoke to Zabek's mother again about five minutes ago to let her know her daughter's stuff had been taken in as evidence, save her coming over to the UK just yet. She mentioned Zabek's house. It's all bought and paid for and is now standing abandoned. The mother wanted to keep it, again in case Zabek returned."

Bethany got chills. "Shit. Do you think this George . . . ?"

"I don't know, but it's worth going out to check. Claire could be there."

"Okay, we're going now. Message Mike the address, because I'll be driving."

She jammed her phone away, told Mike what Fran had said, and they legged it out of the station and into the car.

Flooring it, adrenaline doing a number on her, she careened down the street, blue lights flashing, keeping the siren off.

Mike accessed his messages. "Calding Lane."

She headed there, her mind swirling, and about half a mile from it, she gasped. Closer now, the car hurtling along, she made out the skeleton of a house, and a fire engine.

"Fuck me," Mike said. "If Claire was in there . . ."

"I don't even want to think about it."

At last, she pulled up behind the fire engine and got out to speak with the one person she'd been avoiding all this time.

"Cuppa." She smiled and gave him a hug.

"It's bloody good to see you." He drew back and let her go.

"What do we have here?" she asked, making it clear this was work, not time for a friendly natter.

"Looks like arson to me. There's a body. Pretty charred, so I'm afraid there isn't a visual you can go on. None you'd want to see anyway." Cuppa winced. "We'll have to wait for the inspector to have a nose at it for a final cause, but that's my initial findings. I've tackled enough fires to know it was started in the back room, ground floor, debris piled around the body."

"Can you tell if it's a man or woman?" she asked.

"Nope. Like I said, too charred."

She thought about Vinny and how he'd have looked the same come the end. She had to push the image out of her head and not glance over at the building with its collapsed walls and someone burnt to death.

She thanked Cuppa, waved off his suggestion of getting together for a drink, and got back in the car. Mike joined her and pointed ahead.

"Car. Ford. I'll ring it in," he said.

Bethany did a three-point turn and got the hell out of there, the smell of smoke and the sight of devastation too much.

What the hell did you go through, Vin?

She concentrated on driving, going back to Shadwell in the opposite direction to where they'd come. The road was long and eerily empty, the area perfect for a perverted teacher to do those terrible things to the children in her care. They'd have to contact the school and ask them to get hold of all former pupils who might need therapy. Awful.

"The car's down as stolen a month ago," Mike said. "And as it's still at the scene, I'm hoping to God it's this George who's dead. If it isn't, surely he'd have driven it away."

"Not necessarily. Maybe Claire was his last victim and he had no use for the car anymore. The fucker must have kept an eye on Zabek's house all these years and decided to use it. To think that Stacey and Helen were probably taken there and he burnt their skin, killed them in the house of his former abuser — and there's no doubt in my mind he was abused as well."

"Finding him is going to be a nightmare."

"It is, but we have to. We can't let him do this to anyone else."

"If he had intentions of repeating this, wouldn't he have kept the house? It's in an ideal place, where no one would know what was going on."

"Makes me wonder why he didn't just bury Stacey and Helen there. I mean, I understand why he wouldn't with Zabek. She might have been discovered when the movers took all her stuff to storage."

"Maybe he wanted them in the woods with Zabek. He might have been recreating the past, told himself Stacey and Helen *were* Zabek, know what I mean?"

"Yep, but if that isn't Claire in that house, where is she?" She slapped the steering wheel. "Would he have had the balls to bury her in the woods, knowing we've been there so recently? Christ, we don't even know if that bloke with the body-finding equipment is still there. Or Claire could be buried in another part of the woods instead. That body at the house could be another missing woman . . ." The possibilities were endless and they stuffed themselves inside her head so she couldn't think straight.

"Don't panic. I'll ring in to get some uniforms out there. They can walk the whole lot and see if any ground has been disturbed."

She nodded, breathed out slowly. "Right." An inhale. "Right."

At the station, she parked and hoofed it indoors, heading for the stairs.

"Beth, wait!" Rob called. "I was just about to ring you."

She stopped dead and turned to face him, bumping into Mike's side. "What?"

"There's someone in the soft interview room to see you."

Fucking hell, she didn't need this now. "Who?"

He smiled, obviously of a mind to play games. She wasn't, and before she bit his head off, she stomped through the doorway and flung the interview room door open. The duty doctor jumped a mile and spun to look at Bethany and Mike, shielding the person on the armchair. Bethany moved to the side so she could peer around, and shock stole her breath.

"Claire?"

She was a state, her hair bedraggled, her lips chapped. And her arms . . . He'd burnt her like he'd burnt Stacey and Helen, and Bethany thanked whoever was up there looking out for this woman, because the next step would have been Claire getting stabbed in the torso. Dying. Being buried.

Goosebumps ran riot over her skin, and Bethany gaped, relief bounding through her, and she walked forward. Claire stood and crumpled onto Bethany, sobbing against her chest.

"Oh God, you poor woman," Bethany said, unashamed that she cried along with Claire. "What the hell did he do to you?" She eased her onto the sofa and sat beside her, holding her hands. "Where is he?"

"In a house. He set fire to it with the tool he used to burn me." Claire released a shuddery breath. "He went all weird and jabbed his fingers in his eyes, stabbed a pen into his neck. I had to run out, had to leave him there. He said he needed to burn, that I should stay and burn with him. Oh God, and he had my knickers on, the ones with the holly all over them. I *said* he stole them; I *knew* he had."

More relief winged its way into Bethany's limbs, and they felt weak, heavy. The bastard was dead. Not Claire. Not some other woman. But the mention of holly on the knickers . . .

"What were the knickers like?" Bethany asked.

"Red, with holly all over and a green ribbon on the front."

A green ribbon . . . "Who was it?" Her voice sounded harsher than she'd intended.

"Andrew, my neighbour."

Phillips? My fucking God, I was right all along.

"Does he also go by the name of George?" Bethany held her breath.

Claire shook her head. "I don't know." A pause. "But he mentioned a George Bernard Shaw play. He . . . he made me get undressed and press my front to his back. Said we had to 'skin'."

Bethany almost gagged at the image of that parading around in her head.

Mike got on the phone, and while Claire cried again, leaning against Bethany, he cancelled the uniforms going to the woods and got hold of Isabelle to join them at Phillips' place.

"We have to go," Bethany said. "To his house. There might be others there. Other women. But I'll be back, I promise, and you can tell me everything. Has anyone contacted your dad?"

Claire nodded. "I asked that he stay away until I've told you what happened."

"Okay." Bethany rose. "I'll see you soon. We'll sort a statement. Then you can go home."

* * *

CLAIRE'S SCENARIO

Necessity: Blame it all on thy neighbour.

NEEDED:
A STRONG WILL TO MAINTAIN INNOCENCE
A BELIEF THAT YOU DID THE RIGHT THING
THE COURAGE TO SEE IT THROUGH UNTIL THE END

'Then you can go home.'

So they're letting you leave then. Later. Once you've told your tall tale in all its glory.

You sit there after that nice police lady has left and wonder whether you were convincing enough. Whether you seemed genuine. Whether your little lies had sounded like the truth. Your tears, though, they were genuine.

And it's plausible, what you said. He *could* have gouged at his own eyes, stabbed at his neck.

Has the Sharpie melted, fused with his body?

Probably.

You think about the complaints you've made, how it's all down on paper that this man was a creep, obsessed by you, and that alone should give credence to your version of events.

Can you live with yourself after what you've done? Can you carry the burden of this secret to your grave, never telling a soul what really happened? That you planned this murder after reading Scenario Eighteen? That you became a killer by choice?

Yes, I can.

Bonus! Spiffing, darling!

CHAPTER TWENTY-ONE

The journey to Andrew Phillips' was fraught with tension. What if they found another woman there? Bethany thought about when they'd previously visited Phillips, going inside even. Mike had checked it, the loft as well, and no one else had been there, but what if Phillips had abducted someone after that?

"Oh God," she said.

"What?" Mike turned to look at her.

"I just remembered something Phillips said. About there being nothing in his loft but yellow fluff. Then what Ian Oliveson said about Zabek telling him if he stepped on the insulation, he'd fall through and die. Was that why Phillips had said that? You know, you going in the loft bringing back memories, and he blurted it out?"

"We'll never know, will we." He scrubbed at his chin. "But yeah, nothing in the loft, as in, there's no kid tied to the bloody rafters having a woman abusing him. She was some messed-up bitch. Makes me sick to my stomach. I'm glad she's bloody dead."

She agreed and parked outside the house, behind the SOCO van, and glanced at Claire's lovely new front door, then at Phillips' place. All the curtains had been drawn, likely on Isabelle's say so. It saved nosy neighbours seeing what was going on inside. And some of those neighbours were out having a look-see, including Ginny, who stood in her garden. She stared across at Bethany, wringing her hands.

Bethany got out and approached her.

"Claire . . . ?" Ginny's eyes watered. "Is she . . . ?"

"She's safe."

"Oh, thank God. *He* went out earlier, and I thought . . ." She thumbed the air at Phillips' house. "I was tempted to follow him, because I'm convinced he has something to do with it."

"He's presumed dead." Bethany wasn't going to fob this woman off. She'd clearly been worrying. "He won't be coming back."

"Was it . . . ? Did he . . . ?"

"Claire will probably tell you when she's home, but if I can offer a bit of advice, let her come to you. She's been through a lot and has quite a bit to process and get over."

Ginny nodded. "I understand. God, I hope she's okay."

"She will be."

Bethany patted her arm then signed the log at Phillips' front door, giving Tory Yates a nod. Mike had already gone inside. In the hallway, she togged up then wandered around, the furniture and ornaments on the ground floor even more obvious now that he'd fashioned his home the same as Zabek's. That woman must have really fucked him up.

She took the stairs and started with the spare room, seeing as no one else was in there yet, and stared in bewilderment at a black paper cutout of a female silhouette taped to the wall. Small maps had been drawn on it in silver, and above each one were words showing what they were: THAT WOMAN'S HOUSE. THE COMMUNITY CENTRE. CLAIRE'S HOUSE. HELEN IN THE WOODS.

Grey diamond-like patterns covered the rooms in That Woman's House and The Community Centre, while it rested beneath trees at the woods. Bethany shuddered, realising what it was. She studied the back of her hand, and the same pattern was there. Skin. Probably belonging to Zabek, Stacey, and Helen.

One hell of a sick bastard.

A shout went up from somewhere, and Bethany dashed out onto the landing and into the other bedroom. Mike stood by a chest of drawers, head to toe in protective gear, a pile of women's knickers in his gloved hands. A SOCO peered over and grunted his disgust.

"I expect they all belong to Claire," Mike said and riffled through the stack.

"Those ones look a bit old-fashioned." She moved towards him. The pair in question were a bronze colour, possibly fake silk parading as real, a thick band of lace at the waist. "Might be Zabek's."

"Providing he hasn't washed them, testing might prove it. Depends on whether they can get a sample off them after all this time." Mike bagged the garments. "Not that it matters anymore now that they're dead. It's just for the file, closing the case."

Bethany thought of the hairbrush found at The Big Red Box and hoped forensics would find something on those bronze beauties to match it with Zabek. She'd been a foul woman, ruining Andrew, turning him into someone just as foul.

What would he have turned out like had she not got her hands on him?

While everyone else mooched around the rest of the house, Isabelle and her team dusting for prints — who knew if Stacey or Helen had been brought here? — and searching in cupboards and drawers, Bethany returned to the spare room. She looked out of the window, and there, in the corner of the garden, was a camera on a tripod, illuminated by the light coming from the house to the right. It was pointing towards Claire's. What had he been doing recording her? What did he expect to capture on film? Maybe his infatuation with the woman meant any footage would do, so long as he could stare at her on his TV screen.

Isabelle came in and stood beside her. "Forgot to tell you. There were some photos in with Zabek's belongings. Some kid or other standing in front of a window, and either side were mannequins. They had the dresses on."

Bethany whipped her head round. "What, the Victorian and renaissance?"

Isabelle nodded. "And the boots, ballerina shoes, and they were holding those little velvet bags."

"So he stole them off her after he'd killed her."

"Clearly had a thing about them."

"He had a thing about a lot." Bethany told her about Claire's holly knickers. "So we can only assume he put the holly and ribbon on the plastic bags in the graves because they were something to do with Claire. She was someone he wanted, for whatever reason, and he zoomed in on her, stealing her underwear, doing the stalking, and now this camera." She pointed at the garden.

"Bloody hell." Isabelle exhaled. "And what's this load of old cobblers?" She turned to look at the silhouette.

"If you study it for long enough, you'll work it out for yourself."

Isabelle stepped closer. "Oh, that's not skin, is it?" She shivered. "I wonder if the skin on those flames in that champagne glass belongs to Zabek."

"We'll soon find out. Pisses me off that I don't know the significance of the glass, though. Why was it broken? Why were the flames put in there?"

"With Phillips presumed dead, the truth of that has died with him."

Bethany sighed. "It has, and part of me is relieved. Do I *really* want to know what explanation he'd come up with? I don't think so. Given the weirdness of this case, I imagine it's something I'm better off not being aware of." She gestured to the silhouette. "That cutout will have some reason to it as well."

"Maybe that's how he saw Zabek. A black shape. Like a monster."

Bethany huffed out a breath. "But he was a monster himself."

"He probably didn't see it that way. She must have broken his little boy brain, and that's just awful."

His sister, Dalene, sprang into Bethany's mind, and she messaged Ursula on the front desk, seeing as time had moved along and Rob would have left. She'd sent Fran and Leona home. No point in them staying late now. Things could wait until tomorrow.

> Bethany: CAN YOU GET ME THE PHONE NUMBER FOR DALENE PHILLIPS IN LONDON?

"I'll have to speak to his sister," Bethany said to Isabelle, "tell her there's a strong possibility he might be dead." She also wanted to get the woman talking about Andrew.

Ursula replied, supplying the landline number.

Isabelle smiled. "I'll leave you to it. We'll be here a while yet, but there's no reason for you to hang about. See you when I see you."

Bethany nodded and called Dalene, expecting a frosty reception again.

The woman answered with a bark of, "Who is this?"

"Hi. It's DI Bethany Smith from the Shadwell police. We called before about your brother, Andrew. I'm afraid I have some bad news. A body was found after a fire in the property of a lady called Estera Zabek and—"

A quick inhale then a gasp cut Bethany off.

"Is it him?" Dalene asked.

"We believe so."

"Good."

That took Bethany aback. "Miss Phillips, can you explain why this isn't upsetting you? It's your brother."

"He deserves to be dead after what he told me he did."

"What did he do?"

"I don't want to talk about it."

"If you know something, it's better to tell me. If you've been keeping any secrets for him . . ."

A mirthless laugh, sharp and cutting. "He stole Miss Zabek's knickers. Sorry, but he went weird when he was about ten, and I kept my distance as much as I could."

With nothing else forthcoming, Bethany wound the call up. She wasn't going to heap any more on her shoulders. This would make the national papers if Uxbridge managed to sell an article, his police informant giving him all the gory details. Dalene would hear all about it then. For now, she could wallow in ignorant bliss.

Phone away, and God, she hoped it wouldn't ring again this evening. She left the room and got Mike. Drove them to the station. A note had been left from Fran. Helen's and Stacey's phone records. Bethany had a quick read and could only surmise that Phillips had pretended to be Stacey in some conversations with Helen.

Devious bastard.

They had a few hours left of the evening yet to question Claire. They wanted to get the interview out of the way sooner rather than later so the poor woman could attempt to move on with her life. Bethany would have to get hold of Claire's father later, ask him to collect her. He had the keys to the new front door.

First, a cup of coffee and a five-minute sit-down with Mike so they could decompress before hearing the details of Claire's terrible experience. Then it'd be home time, a quick meal, and bed.

God, how she longed for that.

A message came from Isabelle.

Isabelle: HELEN'S LAPTOP FOUND AT PHILLIPS', PLUS STACEY'S PHONE.

Bethany sighed. It was far from over. So much yet to do. Paperwork. Tying up loose ends. Still, tomorrow was another day.

* * *

CLAIRE'S SCENARIO

Necessity: Keep your story straight. Always.

It takes three hours to tell them what happened, most of it the truth, the rest white lies. Or big old black lies, but that's what you have to do. For the rest of your life. Stick to the same story, over and over.

When you see Dad, you crumble, wanting so much to tell him you got rid of 'the dickhead', as he's so fond of calling him. But you don't. You stick to what you told the woman detective — "Please, call me Bethany, not Mrs Smith." — and the man — "Same here. It's Mike."

They'd let you go with assurances you could contact them at any time if you recalled anything else, but you won't remember a thing unless it means getting you out of the shit later if forensics, that fire inspector, or the coroner find something that proves you didn't tell the truth.

You'll deal with that as and when. Maybe have a convenient loss of memory.

The duty doctor disinfected your burns, put a salve on, and bandaged them up — you refused to go to the hospital tonight, even though second-degree burns were mentioned, and some other kind of burn you can't remember. It's bad, will need grafts, but that's a problem for another day. You promised them you'd go tomorrow, let the nurses have a proper look. The duty doctor gave you painkillers. Strong ones. You'll take them before bed. Hopefully you'll sleep all night. The nightmares you used to have about him will change. They'll no longer be about a stalker, but perhaps him burning you, and you burning him.

Time will tell.

For now, you're at home, Dad leaving you be, and even though it's late, you drop a quick message to the girls at Books & Bags, then go outside into your garden and sit in your usual spot, placing your bag on the table with a thermos of tea inside, a snack or two if you get peckish. He won't come out and dance in his garden or climb over the fence and waffle on about plays. He'll never encroach on your personal space again. Never steal your knickers. Never follow you places. Never do anything except rot.

You take your Kindle out and fire it up. Twenty percent battery where you'd read while waiting for Bethany and Mike to come back from Andrew's and begin the interview. You close *One Hundred Ways to Kill Thy Neighbour*. There's no point in reading it now, is there. Instead, you select a Tudor book by Phillipa Gregory and prepare to lose yourself in the world of years gone by, Henry Eighth at his wicked best.

Someone interrupts, though, coming out of Andrew's back door, and for a moment you freeze, thinking it's him. Forgetting he's no longer there. A white forensic suit seems to float without a body in it, down to the bottom of the garden, to the camera on its tripod. The faint red light of it recording glows, and you stare at where you imagine the lens is and smile.

You're free, sweetheart. Completely free.

THE END

THE JOFFE BOOKS STORY

We began in 2014 when Jasper agreed to publish his mum's much-rejected romance novel and it became a bestseller.

Since then we've grown into the largest independent publisher in the UK. We're extremely proud to publish some of the very best writers in the world, including Joy Ellis, Faith Martin, Caro Ramsay, Helen Forrester, Simon Brett and Robert Goddard. Everyone at Joffe Books loves reading and we never forget that it all begins with the magic of an author telling a story.

We are proud to publish talented first-time authors, as well as established writers whose books we love introducing to a new generation of readers.

We have been shortlisted for Independent Publisher of the Year at the British Book Awards three times, in 2020, 2021 and 2022, and for the Diversity and Inclusivity Award at the Independent Publishing Awards in 2022.

We built this company with your help, and we love to hear from you, so please email us about absolutely anything bookish at: feedback@joffebooks.com.

If you want to receive free books every Friday and hear about all our new releases, join our mailing list: www.joffebooks.com/contact

And when you tell your friends about us, just remember: it's pronounced Joffe as in coffee or toffee!

ALSO BY EMMY ELLIS

DI BETHANY SMITH

Book 1: THE COLD CALL KILLER
Book 2: THE CREEPY-CRAWLY KILLER
Book 3: THE SCREWDRIVER KILLER
Book 4: THE SCORCHED SKIN KILLER

DETECTIVE CAROL WREN MYSTERIES

Book 1: SPITE YOUR FACE
Book 2: HOLD YOUR BREATH
Book 3: GUILT BURNS HOLES
Book 4: BEST SERVED COLD
Book 5: BLOOD RUNS DEEP

Printed in Great Britain
by Amazon

37992258R00108